INFINITY IN FINITY

IN BITS

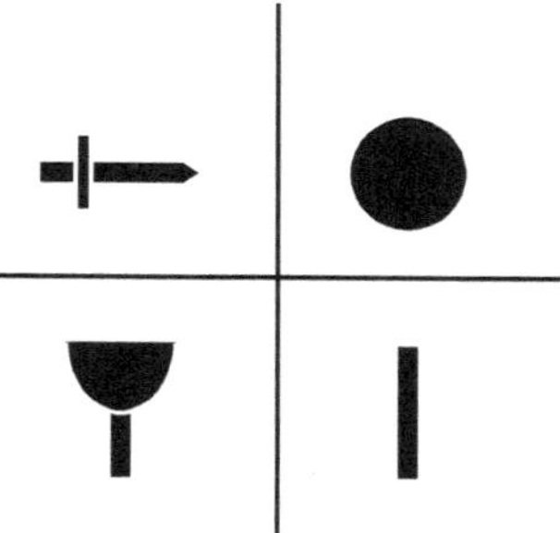

INFINITY IN BITS

Michael J. Rowland

ISBN 978-1-9996964-7-4

Equus Press
Birkbeck College (William Rowe), 43 Gordon Square, London,
WC1 H0PD, United Kingdom

Typeset and design by Jo Blin & Michael Rowland
Printed by Tigris

The publisher wishes to acknowledge the support of James H. Ottaway, Jr.

Composed in 10pt Caslon, composed by William Caslon in 1734.

For Jo and Chantelle

"How does one write a book about the Tarot?
It is like trying to empty the sea with a fork."

—Marianne Costa

CONTENTS

MAJOR ARCANA

00
THE FOOL

You got me mixed up with someone who thinks he knows who he is.

So oh no you don't, you hold on there, MissMister! You got hands where your knees should be and ears where your feet are, and your words are all sun–blistered. And I'm not in love, I'm not in anything.

Betty Page kicked us out of her yard party and so here you find me slowing down to pick up my pace and lunge. Lunged.
Your soft laugh won't make me grow none. I am one, and I am alone, which negates the one and leaves me none until your teeth fall out with age and the light you light on them's done gone.
You got him mixed up with me and her mixed up with him.
You oughta be more careful where you shake that stick, my friend.

J'ai suivi

The answer is you. You are more the fool. Always. Don't even doubt it. Betty's was a blast, but she expected too much from this gadfly and his blue–faced pet.

"Who you calling pet, kimosabe?"
"You, you fool."

We are both being followed. Still. By my Thunderbird. By my broad–winged eagle spirit.
It is I, up there and down here, and that is why we are leaving, my friend.

"Mat, man, sister, babe, brother! I don't know what you are talking about half the time."

"I apologise. You, you are my better half. Never stop talking to me. I need you now more than ever before. And there have been many befores before this. So where do we go?"

April 30th, Čarodějnice, Holešovice, Prague – for example.

Where we can all see in the dark.
The universal superpower revealed.
The 'Nothing' destroyed the instant it was created.
And the only explanation we can find?
Love heals.
Love kills.
And it's as daft as a bleach enema.

2020 visionaries plagiarising nature's cryptic algorithms.

One by one,
Get one free.
The sun–dried lectures and Caiparhinas on me!
That should keep us going till 3033.

"Excuse me, miss, do you feel patriotic?"
Do I feel what?!
"Patriotic."
What do I even look like to you? You painted, plaited, forty–coated, hominid.

– We act not for ourselves but for all mankind.
– Life isn't about finding yourself; life is about creating yourself.
– I took all the money I had and paid for everything out of my own pocket.
– I didn't get where I am today...

Nobody's got anything to say on the matter of saying things that matter if they's depending on the presumption that words matter!
A fucking patriot!! I'll give you patriot!

Hey! I'm a big man and I know what I want.
I've got a big guitar and I know what I want.
I've written this thing for our country. A new national anthem.

The crescendo of the song is a masturbating Mobius Strip that murders all the snowflakes who don't sing along. The genre? Rapey jazz. The Purpose?

Unite and divide.

The wide blue laptop screens and hard naked totems
reminiscent of Walpurgis Nacht and the stygian witches' promise to make
the infinite visible.

It's a myth that the government looks out for you.
It's a myth that art has meaning.
It's a myth that eating carrots helps you see in the dark.
And it's a myth that joy has a ceiling.

I'm proud to have all my own teeth and I'm proud to be able to live on my
own without fearing the on–come of inevitable insanity, and proud also to
be welcoming blackness with a squirrel's strong arms.

Can a rabbit look in a squirrel's eyes and say, "I forgive you all of your
differences. I respect your culture and your burrowing and the speed with
which you cover incredible long grassy distances"?

You know it's called 'Having a squirrel' when you have a monkey on your
back? Everyone should wear a mask. The truth comes out when you know
you can hiiiiide from the rodent insiiiiide.

Kinoscope collages. Tyko's special knowledge of the underworld and Lou-
is' penchants and Jaromír's trenches and Marko's bulbs watered like a circus.

Pete Seeger pulled his pants on and stared at the TV.

Who's this fella they's all talkin about? Seems he's got all kindsa people
riled.
And I'm dead and my songs meant nuthin' and the world is unsavable?!
And I
Am Dumb.

But I have 20–20 vision and I am looking at Future Pete. And Future Pete
is only three minutes into his story, and he doesn't know where he got this
clear sight from...
Whether it's from World War 2, Vitamin A,

Or his openness to considering that he might be gay,
Or his freedom to plan how he'd do himself in,

Or his spread–legged gait from all that folksy, witchy sin.

Day 56

Two more bottles might not be enough

And we really should consider our weight

But the comfort food is comforting

And the beer's an anaesthetic

And the fear is magnetic

And everything is irrelevant in the face of what we're dealing with on a
day-to-day Ginsberg.

A young skinny Ginsberg.
Got his eyes on the prize Ginsberg.

Fuck all that old poetry and Ginsberg.
Ginsberg was never skinny,
Not even when he was born
Which was daily,

Laughing fatly,
Reading the Kaddish to a bingo room full of oldies and curtained, plaid
vaginas.

Maybe we will see you once–again–forever.

And the takeaway from all this?
I don't want it ever to end.
Long live the never ending.
Long live the infinite.
Long live the all-seeing
carrot.

01
THE MAGICIAN

It will be created in my words.

And smell like a lap dancer in a petrol station or a lumberjack playing tennis.

And it will taste like wine and chocolate.

And look like words.

And feel like a bear hug from a friend.

And sound like waves, and leaves, and you.

It will be the trinity of infinity, infinity and infinity. Two infinities too many plus anything else you can imagine in your toll booth to the stars as you sit with your naked back to me, and watch the passengers go by in driverless vehicles, and you confiscate their pocket money and switch-blades and gear sticks and lemonades and wish you were there in the back seat playing 'I Spy' or some such silliness to kill the time till you reach your goal and disappear your cumulus goats.

"You don't look a day over 1."
"Oh, go on."

It will add up to 365 and rhyme with orange and save up for a rainy day and eat porridge for breakfast and climb Mount Everest and calculate the nearest point to Pi.

It will jump over its knees and praise the ease of everything which is price-less. It will work hard at relaxing and throw at you all the positive it has. It will make its own cakes and eat them. It will create its own competitors

GILBERT
Sto
Leiber
RNER
BERNSTEIN
LOWE.
OR

and beat them. It will invite royalty to dinner and seat them. And it will see troubles coming from a mile off and greet them with switchblades and lemonades.

I Spy with my third eye something beginning with Aleph.
A pussy cat? A puppy dog? A crocodile? A tortoise?

#yesyesathousandtimesyes

"Promise me, Mummy, you'll never die."
"I promise, cherub. I promise, my clever little man."

It will be below as it is above; quark soup for 'The Splendid Generation'.
Seedless grapes, parties without hangovers, five-hour orgasms, categorical imperatives, unarmed guards, ready–grated cheeses, no Mohammed, no Buddha, no Moses, no Jesus,
just one long game of 'witch and wizard chess' where you control your actions and perform your art undressed.

The music of the Fool plays on and gathers momentum as it skateboards along the sword of your intellect, as it massages gently the cups of your breasts, as it tightrope walks steadily across the shaft of your arrow and disappears into the ocean blue of your iris
and from within
will try its very best
to square the ibis.

The four senses – The four suits – The specky four eyes
Four arms?
Forearms?
For arms?
Or
For alms?
Alms.

Slam! 8 knocked on its side. The purity of a _salm with a silent, invisible P. Look me up next time you come round. I will be the one. The tom–boyish one with the new hairdo. Again again. For you. You never notice. But that's okay. You have a lot on your plate and a long way to go. Now on with the show, Peter Pan, on with the show.

FEDS YOU
1 2 3
G'NIGHT
White Pride
OPPOSITE
CHAIR

02
THE HIGH PRIESTESS

Clouds to the left of me, Joker to the right.

Familiars full of grace shielding me against the cold, blue desert night.

"The artist of your bodyblessing." (Second through brain) – Hidden in vain
Mummy long Legs coquettishly crossed till it's time to reveal the sacred velvet labyrinth.
And you thank me for all I do, but it's not for you. Not yet. You must earn it. And for that you must learn it. But I alone translate the book of secrets. The words which can free you.

The Epic of Peace is seeded within me, but Godlessly present. Put there by a chancer. A peasant.

Until you can riddle me this, you must invent your own prizes and you'll take it and like it till you see with your very own eyes that godlessness which resists, exists.
Worship me meanwhile. My foot on your moon–shaped head. My eyes on your soul. My eyelids tickling your foot on my soul. One more time a BJ. One more time a granite girl. A pomegranate girl.

In your strength you shall establish 2. Release your finger from the trigger there is nothing to fear, I am going nowhere, I am the bosom of the world, and I can rap faster than Superman Spiderman Batman Wolverine Hulk and The Flash combined! OH YEEAAHHH!

I will be a giantess.

I will be an Empress.

I will be a force to be reckoned with; a poly–platonic Persephone gargling eternal recurrence from praying card to praying card, liquidised string theories rehearsed by an open–hearted dramaturge.

At the day of great peace, I will become one with thee, as Zero becomes one with Two.

Once you have consciously affected Tiphareth, these streamings will become evident and you will not need my books or my good looks any longer.

Only that which kills you, makes you stronger.
Walk! Walk blindly, foolishly, misguidedly. The path is the thing. The path and the occasional pomegranate.

03
THE EMPRESS

Thanks for your interest, Carla. I am sending a photo and text of one of twenty-one, which I think will frankly blow the others out of the water. Lux and Lydia capacitated by H.P. Source.

She sometimes gets the urge to kiss people in strange places; this is her prerogative. As I see it she is of the Louvre oeuvre, grand and grandiose with a six-foot tear in her dress.

She is a 'free woman', orange–pinnacled glad–rag Charleston + Champagne.
Mister! Youse be ladled down on a watery waterbed with enough fuel for all seven chakras and a little left over for the shadow babies.

A Wasteland filled with Lux's visions; famous clairvoyant learnt her words off by heart. Now the performance can start. Kaleidoscopic Ceorl, the unveiled placenta shared in rhyme; come and have a go if you think you're hard enough....when you're hard enough.

Russ Meyer reversed – the Russ who wasn't cursed by an obsession with large breasts and a penchant for violence. Russ the artist. Russ the philosopher. Russ the poet. Reborn Dawn of the Idols.
Since Lux is the door there is no difference between inside and outside. Her world is a shared digital garden of joyful abundance. Honestly, Carla, I think she would be perfect for the role.

She started life as a triangle but she's willing to be framed in a square, seated at the delta–Maher apex protrudes beyond your well–meaning limitations. She is the great Mother, and her borders lie beyond your Nielsen ratings. Your programming is a tomb, and my client is the womb. Her mind a cosmic clitoris, her vagina the tent flap to a whole TARDIS of Prakriti Graffiti.

She is the path of illuminating intelligence – the universal subjective mind, so she is asking higher rates than most since there are no other candidates of her kind anywhere. And you'll be happy to pay the extra when you see her. No, I lay odds you will want to BE her!

Wishes come in triplets
On a daily basis.
If days to you all look the same
You're clearly a day racist.

She may appear green to you, but she has been here before
All the colours can be found in her greenness if you look closely;
She's the new white, don't you know.

"I'll bet she's a real YoYo."

Yeah, she says she loves you too.

Look, if you don't pin this one down this time round someone else is going to swoop in and grab her. Chances like this come once an aeon, and aeons don't grow on trees. Just between you and me this could be the last one, so do yourself a favour and cuddle in nice and cosy next to her. And you should know something. Get ready. She's a hugger.

Celebrate your sensual side – touch yourself. Touch yourself in strange places. She would.

04
THE EMPEROR

Hobbs
Head of b—b—b—bank security.
Stable. Solid. S.S.

Hobbes. 3 Days since meltdown. No promise of an atmosphere tomorrow.
No promise of tomorrow.
Take your eyes off the prize and look to the skies.
Emperor = MC.
Square Artificial Throne.
The daughter is the father of the man.
4 hobs. Same as your face.
No exit.
We are in it for the legacy.
The fire keeps on burning.
The Phoenix reborn.

Samo Samo but different. The Threshold hard-wired into the mainframe.
Twenty-one lock codes.

Mine, a trifle. I do it for the logic. There is a god in the logic.

The material my mettle. Technology's tentacles tattooing 'Love is a weakness' on the Empress's backside along with a number.
Angel 3394.
One more me would be too many. An 'Overbearing bastard!' she called me.

3+3+9+4 = 19
1+9 = 10
1 + 0 = 1

The door you have not noticed before will be unlocked when your interest
in material goods is replaced by a deeper interest in self.
You can't hallucinate the past except when you think about it.

You were and always will be a genius, and when your intellect diminishes
and you retire beneath your rock, the sun will praise you for staying the
distance.

The bronco you bucked from your broken old back for those gold topped
trees you liked so much; cowboy of the suburbs with basic needs thought
of who it was laid the first brick down in famous churches.

You are at war with fragility.

This here is where we interrupt today's broadcast with a ram, with her
light, with L. Two Ls. This here is where we start building.
With or without you.

Gilded ideas. A rehearsal scene carved in stone. Carved with confidence. "See, everything is just so black and white with you. Like words. In words the power. No power in the grey. No pwr. Les pr.

1111
????
I cannot connect with you in mothers' light .
I connect when I don't fight.
You don't fight when I don't fight.
Wr alrt.

I.M. Interior Ministry.
I.M.
I am.

I Am has sent me to you.
Ehyeh asher eh yeh. This is what he told me.
He will be who he will be.
And I create what(ever) I create.
M.I.? M.I.?
The ministry's interior...

...and so to the contrary.

We will always find each other.
All ways.

05
THE HIEROPHANT

Va via Voom!
A long-forgotten question remem-
bered.
Vav.

Just like this.
Not like this.
Goes like that.

Far less to this than meets the eye and the door is closed, and the window shut. Just for the time being that is. Time being what it is.
The ape behind you, a celebrity engine; nature's mechanics in his eyes. The wisdom of a witch–watch and comfortable shoes. The player behaves himself when you speak. Trusts you. Let's himself be guided and bides his lunch breaks reading updates of false gods. Vampire–clad, shoddy todgers muscling up enough venom to spew at your Hieroglyphics; and you.

The director's chair pointing in the right direction. He lifts you tangently to your higher parquet. Two dimensional scripts shifting to three and four and you, if you can keep within the boundaries of common sense, he may set you free and watch you come alive at five.

Vau Vav VOOM!
In this four–walled room. One belief system too soon and you might well dogmatise yourself out of a whole cornucopia of ideals – notforreals – stone roses – lemon peels.

Faith without works is dead. But death still works even without faith.

If the streams cross, we will blow each other to pieces. Take one key each and we'll meet you on the beaches.

Slowdown in order to move faster towards your higher purpose.

"You got a porpoise!? What do you feed it on?"

The ordinary is extraordinary if you take away the imaginary nails.

IRON ONES RAN IN.

...from Limehausens to Jail. Pounding her and joining her, and all for her, and the greater good.
Whether fish or flesh or fairy tales with idols made of wood.
The hidden wisdom unlocked and hung around her neck; that secure sense of falsity until you unscramble your own deck.

U is the means of controlling the energy. V is the U but weighed down with salt.
You are the means of controlling the system; we are the you, but the eye's what we want.

Deity joined to woman.
A pentagramatical synthesis.
Semantics puts itself in the yoke and is willingly led to Atlantis.

Mléčný Zadek.
Supreme Purusha.
Marshmallow mysteries.
Opiate pusher.
He is the source of light.
Your Coke is almost empty.
Your oranges are filthy.
Don't worry, I've brought plenty.

The seeker and the ignorant
Kneel side by side by side.
The invisible one betwixt the two.
Never bridesmaid, always bride.
I poke my forefinger through the circle made by my forefinger and thumb.
Esoteric symbolism for all that is to come.

06
THE LOVERS

Deep within the madding crowd, a culture born, a jester found, a pleasure dome inaugurated. Loved. Deleted.

A sacred symbol amongst the dirge of wedding song notes in chapel sonics read off the hunchbacks of highborn soldiers and robed in scarecrow's mother's grasp.

Not without your blessing, ma'am.

My cup it runneth over.

Long deported days unedited till the reason shifts regardless, or we can hold hands and rejoice...Bang Bang our heads together in true IS RA EL, Myself, who is like god, contends.

And 21 angels riot.

There is a new sheriff in town.

FLASH!

And like that, within a week we killed your parents and hit the road.

Gabriel. Wait. A formal partnership? A bibulous frenzy commodified.

Ask me. Ask me. Ask me. Ask me. Ask me. Ask me.

Ten numbers – Six aspects. All the beauty progressive in your two eyes only focusing on the path ahead; an exquisite heifer 'neath the cum-drenched sky.

Stupid Cupid never far behind. Out of sight, but never out of mind.

Watch carefully as love's clock unwinds. Gotta be brave and true to be unkind.

Drop your guard. Throw off your chains. Now blow out your brains. See what remains.

The chapters you pencilled in, soaked in another's semen, falling apart and dripping down clown–ridden drains. Your house is now truly empty. You are free to beginagain.

Adamant entropy, the colours strewn from your body–oak and secret past and karmic rituals that expound the law of something none of us have ever seen before.

Today is the anniversary of the first day of the rest of your life.

That's no lady, sir! That's my wife.

A kingdom of spirits commissioned to support you.
Tadaa! To be. To dare to do.
To do what you love.
Step into the new square. Rise now.
Though we are nameless, we are with you all the same.
To be trusted in all our teasing numinous 'its'.

Isn't it a bit like cheating?
No more than us not having to learn how to breathe it isn't, no.
What is love?

Love is a daytime chat show host
Bleeding from a 12-foot hole in the neck
Shuffling his dead grandmother's tarot pack
Insisting on going to hell not heck.

Caption–bubbles bursting in the eyes of those you're dating.

A McDonalds paper bag used when hyperventilating.

A tentacled librarian shushing Armageddons.

A one–armed priest with his hand down his pants at weddings.

A sad kleptomaniac putting things back.

A one-way train racing down the wrong track.

Promiscuous snowflakes coupling in the night
Melting on the tongue of a bat midflight.

A Newborn baby being punished at the gate
For jumping feet first and showing up late.

A nine-sided octagon wondering "what the fuck?"

A six-winged, three-footed, no-headed duck.

A particle accelerator on ta–marzipan.

Kylo Ren in the Ku Klux Klan.

Captain Hook beating on children at a feast.

158 the number of the beast.

A man on the cover of a business magazine
Carrying a copy in the hope that he'll be seen.

A graveyard tricycle chained to the fence
Painted bright pink in support of pretence.

Infinity's algorithm working overtime
With no one there to pay it at the end of the line.

Falling from a ladder in the Scottish Player's tights.

Citizen's arresting features reading them their rights.

The big question nailed in a gallery goers' huff,
"Is that part of the exhibition, or just some stuff?"

07
THE CHARIOT

At the mercy of you and your yet what!

DarkStars Dependent Ltd as I grope my way lyrically, you water my ardour from black nothing to white metal bondage gaining momentum thanks to a quart of gin and the flat earth's incessant spin.

Who wound you up?

You are My Star, found; the well unplugged and all three of us heaven ascendants.

The world is enough; nothing less.
There is nothing less.

My roots from the fourth and fifth leg of the magician's table.
I've been much worse selves.

Pharaoh planets aimed at my cheek. There will be a desert isle. There will be sun. There will be poetry and love and you, my sentient cooling gasses say mass for the gods who put us up to this and for the fools who follow.

A peace sign that looks like a rabbit.
A Segway that sounds like fun.
A team I'm building meticulously
So our club members
number
one.

I want your gold chocolate coins to feed my horses.
I want colourful bow ties and leg bandits.

The photos of you in your car with your bare feet resting up on the dashboard like loose reins. Nobody at the wheel.
Catatonic traffic police.

Stars–truck jalopy dream come true. On the outskirts of a purpose-built freeze–frame – You plied me with drink and I told you everything about how I always wanted to be a deep sea diver in one of those big heavy iron helmets but I just didn't have the sea legs. Skinny imp in a cart. The leads in my own Punch and Judy show. To and fro between all your lips.

Disciplined, I got horse sense enough to keep my utility belt on tight, filled and balanced as a yoni fulcrum lingam.
Even the box that trammels the mindset.
Doubt of self is the means to the end.
Doubt of self is the end to the start of the name to the game has you cash in your chips and relinquish the blame.
And in the square the people gathered

Ready for their road trip.

Bill – He say where we goin'?
Sandy – Him? No.
Betty – Does anyone know where we are going?
Tom – Suleiman.
Suleiman – Yeah?
Andrea – Sulieman, do you know?
Kat – Sulieman!

They left
In increments.

08
JUSTICE

You are a house of stained glass.

A pocketful of frozen posies.
Your bodiesbonesbroke.
A sore lip.
A raw deal happy meal kiss.

A hope.
Still.
Stilled.
Toebonesbroke.

Words hide everything.

"You'll be sorry!" you told me
But now it's you who are sorry

Hipbonebroke.

Wordsconnectingeverything separate everything.

Toebonesandhipbones and sugar milestones in acid rain spittle.
Episodic Olympus reached but not achieved.
Handbonesnotbroke
But brittle.
The good things you had coming
Caught in the craw.
Stammering passion poling the all inclusive mid–life–hope–for–hire.
A dope Popeslap.
Neckbonebroke.
And all the queen's swords and all the queen's wands couldn't do harm or
magic to nuthin'.

I put the movie 'Cabaret' on and everyone in it was broken like you
And everybody got what was coming to them
like you.
Like you said would happen with me.
Now look.
Words are hidden in everything.
And say nothing and your surface cuts and bruises suggest broken things
and the blood in the rain suggests internal bleeding but the sugar in your
bones is so so delicious.
So nothing to fix so.

You were wrong
And I was right.
See,
I told you
Words heal everything.

09
THE HERMIT

One direction home and a six–pointed forefinger hand. Gotta light? Gotta light?

In and out of the shadows (you create all on your lonesome) Waddling backwards like some extant Atlantean opportunist.

Lostandfound.

A journey of a thousand miles ends with one step.

No more time wasting at the next station. The next station will be the one. The only stop where the endless possibilities unite and give purpose to light.
Meaning and plot erased.
All accessories outer–spaced.
All advice maced.
Graffitied love notes to the stars written in iron–railway–track–like planetary scars.
A torn paper heart hides beneath your well–worn windcheater trash cans as full as the signposts are illegible.

I, Prince Hal await my judgement. The wheel of Justice prevailing to beckon me.
The time has come for us to consider success.
There is no Harry Percy. There never was. These feuds were man–made. Your love is not.

We are not recruited.

směr Kolín →

We are merely the unslain.
We are royal.
We fathers, mothers, daughters, sons, masters and mentors.
The whoring fools who know.
Your blood in my helmet.
Your light in my fire.
In front of you all
I stand alone and think.
A considered privation
Which none of us own.

We,
My friends,
Are not alone.

I can do no more as a simple parish priest.
I can do no more as a simple man of the earth.
I can do no more as shepherd to my own soul.
I hand it over to you.
Coincidences do not exist.

El Sul – El Sulphur – El Mercuria
Cal El.
I know Apollo; those glasses, that smile. I loved him and you would too, if
only you weren't so afraid of heights.

"It never ends. It just goes on and on..."
Sent to the mountains –
Killing kindness – Prayer beads made of sharks' teeth.
It never ends. It just goes on and on…

The Golden Key is to arrive at no conclusion – no last step.
Walk backwards from what you have done and you will always end where
you had begun.
In sight of each and every rising and setting sun,
Your shadow behind you and rising to meet you.

We leapt into the fog of the dark street, below zero, neon potravinies,
artificial sanctuaries. We hugged goodbye, till next we would meet and
I thought of the tunnel and the softness of your kiss; something I may
forever miss.
The beauty of the golden key is the 'not knowing'.

That ready fear.
Those fiery biscuits.
"I see now the play so lies that I must play a part."
It's the not knowing and so I walk backwards.
It's the not knowing and so I shine my light in barren places.
It's the not knowing and so I hide my naked frame in these robes until you reveal yourself to me in your full glory and I dare to match you.

43

10
THE WHEEL

You could be having eleven stiff blue–exercise arms and a big banjo phallus and a vagina lined with chocolate cranberries or

alternating elbows or see through teeth and a champagne hot-tub full of naked-as-the-day-they-were-reborn champagne friends, and edible foam D&D broadswords and milkshake flavoured monster trucks or bubble-gum pirate ass cheeks
paddled
for example.
Or with a flippety flap all the scary fish bees nice fish and Nivea soaked money spiders enter running competitions in the merry old land of Oz till the five o`clock chill singes and they scoop up their weary Adidi, have nuts and good cakes and corn dogs for the first time on holiday with siblings by the spider-friendly firesides of their portable human-friendly ottomans.

Dada - mixing things together which don't usually mix and so is poetry and so is love and so are cocktails, fried beer moccasins, absinthean prophelactics and Spongebob Square Pants teaching Krav Maga to tinsel whipped jelly babies and God was fat in his MAGA hat and how we got Corona from a Bat!
Paradise would just be unconsciously genuflecting zombies mixing things which don't seem mixable or else we'd all be okay with what we already have and heaven would just be
a pub
or a bus
or a shop that sells Welsh love spoons and French 'amsters.
So you see so you see so surrealism and Pope-Pope-Poe poetry is our best bet at achieving the almighty glibbedy gloop, like hands made of jam or a Rolls Royce which runs on Deja Vu or Brian Cox's happy tears or rings on your fingers and bells on your toes and JayJay's wife, Nora Barnacle was a Mulligan joke, for example.
This will be the kit, this will be it, when there's no tunes left, I'll hold you tightly, there'll be snow underfoot, and warm green grass, and you never looked better, and doo wop is sitting cross legged on a Santa shaped bean bag whispering your next book to you through a megaphone connected to your Mother's maiden name dipped in beautiful petrol so you can get that sweet heady aroma of early morning gas stations when you are asked for your password's password's password.
"Swordfish!"
For example.

Everything that we already have is flowing and there are no restrictions. Stop protesting. Sit still and move these mountains for us would ya. The clusters took our light away. We lower our masks to balance the scales and curse the commercials and their unreasonably January sales.

Or a student's journal stuffed with garlic farmed on Mars in Vampire's bras, matured in jars under dying stars telling sentimental stories in theatre bars,

And a bottle of malt
And a velvet crossbow bolt
In the mitts of seemingly gummy cherubim.

For example.

11
STRENGTH

**There is a lord inside me some-where, A lady in there too.
A jupiter, a Jupiter, A Juno ingenue.
I'm what I'm.**

A lion or a mouse? A lion–mouse.
I am.
In space, I can hear me scream.
Tit for tat – no lion–mouse is going down like that.

IM
AM

We crash landed and here we must stay. Our ship and our memory put to pasture.
"Get word back," was the message – So much for the rapture.
But what with memory loss and buried bones and trickster gods and emerald eyes, she warmed to me, and on her hands and knees crawled to the wreckage moments before a wave the size of Snowdon crashed upon her garlanded head roughly the size of P.J. Proudhon….and she yawns…and his words are nothing….and she now the mother of order.

Between the devil and the page of pentacles there's a moderated sense of enablement;
A glandular flux of
inveigling, modified to suit the unflatterable.

"Open wide! There's someone here to see you."

(15+11 = 26 / 2+6=8)

And my sister's all like "To tame or not to tame, that is the question," and
a little mousey on her shoulder is letting her know how the cumulation of
bespectacled cheddar is beyond and before all cataracts or social contracts.
Death to bad people is not the answer for bad people. Death just is.
How can that be a punishment?

Can you believe it? A man with a history! And I only met him yesterday.
I had him down as a 24-hour kind of guy.
It just goes to show ya!

And her orgasm under the weight of it lasted over an hour like a whale.
So I've heard.

This chasm of rage of spirits of sanity spewing their entrails like well–or-

dered ectoplasm through a spinning colander of Jewish descent and misplaced symbols, all memes and borogoves borrowing dentures for half–cut punchlines and sober retractions.
Words are never haughty if detached from their actions.

A revolution by any other name would be completely misunderstood.

Is underwear inevitable?
Ask Peter and the Wolf.
Is Famine avoidable?
Ask the Nutcracker.

The Russian Lion's definition of consciousness and character, true definitions of entity, individuality, personality and nonentity.

Underwear is not inevitable
and neither is your sanctity.

12
THE HANGED MAN

Audience of One.
He wasn't even embarrassed.

I was kind of embarrassed. I mean it was just him and me in the room. Him on stage and me sitting all on me tod in the audience like that.

He performed the whole one man show for me. The whole thing standing on his head, happy as a clam. There's this painted backdrop canvas of Prague and a 3D tree growing out the side of my eye and Green's green park riddled with yods. And a signpost near the graffiti opposite the speeding ego:

PHILOSOPHICAL GUIDE –

ORGANON (ARISTOTLE)
NOVUM ORGANUM (BACON)
TERTIUM ORGANUM (OUSPENSKY)
THE KEY TO COSMIC CONSCIOUSNESS
THE SPATIAL UNDERSTANDING OF TIME
DO NOT BE LOST IN THE LABYRINTH
OF CONFUSED THOUGHT.

Love truth.

And there's these two kids over the way. Stringy kids. One bending the others ear...

"Said Plautinus to Flakus, 'There are different roads by which the Zen might be reached.' Said Flakus to Plautinus, 'I bet that jerk gets impeached.'"

12.

And the other kid goes, "These symbols of peace and kinship carved from your beautiful feet; there are no secrets from Miss Dobson, and you don't find Zen in the street."

And the three shamans sat dead still in the forest in white robes they did not own in pure white masks they were not wearing, in a clean white marble palace they were not inside. And I knew…

I would free myself from my own hidden shackles, break through that ceiling I built out of ostrich feathers and rabbit glue.
I could finally see
There is nothing to do.

Looking forwards and backwards in time
And seeing it is all the same
Whichever way you look at it.
Therein lies your peace.
In the acceptance of eternal recurrence.
Not in no clumsy hick rhyme.
Now put your gun under your pillow and dream dreams of perfection…

Make peace with uncertainty – No one is sure of nuthin'. If they says they is, they is sellin' sumthin'. Cimrman knew! Cimrman knew! The perfect rhyme is one where the words match exactly. One should only rhyme a word with the exact same word.

Now use your scents.

25   33   452   81
2+5+3+3+4+5+2+8+1 = 33
See.

Next time I'll remember.
Next time I'll remember.

These buckets of patience and oily tides means more than your hair or feet;
your sacrificial feet.
Your specimen of hair we kept wrapped round a toothpick in an alchemical glass tube for the brass and metal pendulum he made which we are to take with a pinch of salty water; the shark was after the drowned phonetician's daughter.

And the first rule of tarotarotarotarota….?
"Fuckin' oughta stay the hell away from things you know nothing about."

Next time I'll remember.
Next time I'll remember.

13
DEATH

Card with no name.

Sex & Death.
Your treasure
muted.
An unknown pulse.
Still.

One down.
3 lucky contestants remain with their lives in their back pockets.
Oh, Death, I love you so.
Do not mention his bony hands. He's shy. They're dry.
No amount of Nivea for men seems to make the slightest bit of difference.
Can't fault his sense of style though.
And his id below the waves, so curvaceous, so alluring. Trained to hold her breath for as long as it takes for Bony Man to think the job has already been done and so he walks away and leaves her alone.
At the bottom of the ocean she plays with her trinkets. The lost treasures from cancelled seasons of the Ship of Fools.

Mystic
NĚCO SEXY.
Vánoční speciál
GODOT
NO PICTURES
Shoes or Sheaths
NO PHOTOS PLEASE
Giddy Up!
PROFITS 47 890

Gold and turquoise and gardening tools.

And death came – but from the outside – like an opinion.

Everybody knows but her – Friends shining a light from a distance – Refracted friends.

….and his parents have bought him a scuba diving suit and breathing apparatus as a graduation present and they convince him to put it on and try it out in their swimming pool in front of his relatives who have come to celebrate his return from college.

He jumps in and sinks down slowly to the bottom and holds onto the lowest rung of the steps to keep himself from floating back up and looks at the distorted shapes looking down at him in the pool wearing his new present and all you can hear is his breathing through the breathing apparatus. So near and so far. So near and so far.

"What do you want, Benjamin?"
"Something different."

A new religion?
No religion?
"Go check your records and see who I am. Am I a god or am I human?"

Seaweed and futons
Clothing black or else no clothes
Clothing black or no light
Sea plants and rubies
MDMA witches
White Light/White Heat
Flippers on your feet

When you go faster it looks like slow motion from here.
"All of our lives are one story told slow, told slower, told to a dead stop."

...and there you are – finally still enough to paint.
I take out my brushes and easel and you remain there, unbudged, fixed; a Happy Princess immortal in my hands. A dead butterfly, but a butterfly all the same.

Except it's one of the generation episodes, thank Newman! What looked like The Doctor's death throws has been phoenixed into a beautiful alien diction – An Alienist speak of genderless boundaries. Kill your television and the companions who no longer serve you and don't forget to switch your phone to silent in a fucking library.

Your work is now to list the distractions which are more than the sum of their parts and calculate their worth in comparison to whatever shoddy goals you have been told to be tied to. You may well learn that you have been planting seeds in a wasteland and craving news from far–flung places the amoeba who surround and suffocate you deride. And here they hide, but you need not.
Decapitate your beliefs and warm yourself in a kitchen of distinction born of Tchaikovsky's destruction.

14
TEMPERANCE

Temperance is a dish best served warm, barefoot and garnished with a healthy amount of merch;

band t–shirts, fridge magnets, posters and C.D.s and shit.
Temperance is not to blame for repetition. Nor is it to be blamed for my inability to say I love you.

Please give me a break...

The devil took my stereo AND my record collection so I'm just finding it a little hard to breathe right now.
Props to the moon.

I told the moon and she told me to shut the fuck up and listen to the dunes.
I trust her but as sure as eggs are chickens she's a mystery that does not want to be solved. I mean I'm no fucking Sherlock Holmes but a donkey on a shed can see we ain't neither of us fit enough for this genre right now.
I mean don't get me wrong, I LOVE the moon...

Sit there! Sit there!
Get away from me!
I need a double seat today.
Read my tee, "Do Not Touch"
A little give and take and we gonna get along just fine.
Not opposite me! Over there!!!

Your words
Like petals from a volcano.

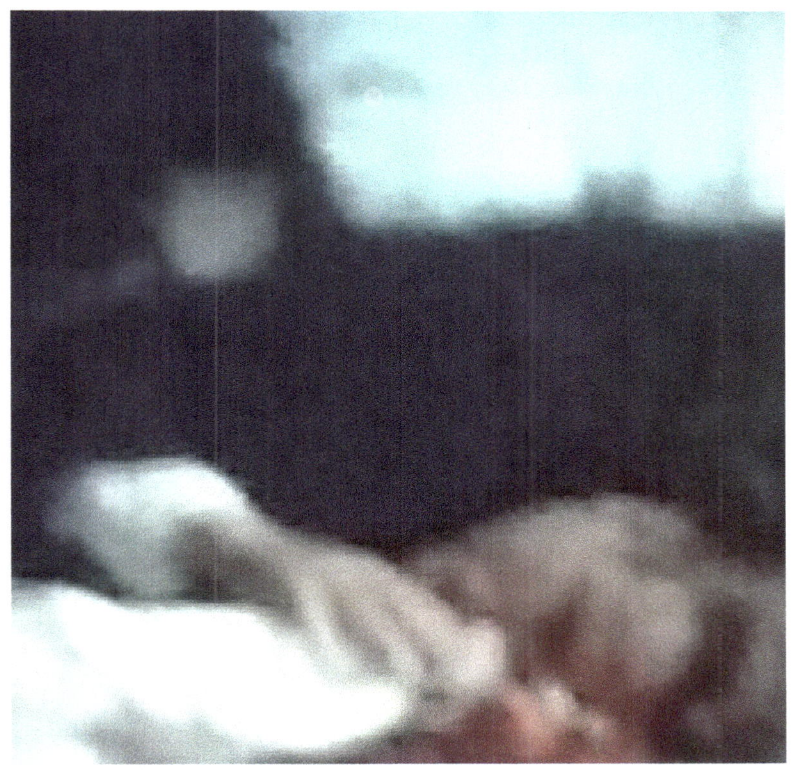

Your body
A tall glass of wine in a tea cosy.

My poetry is becoming
Trite,
Compromised.
I need to be free to spread my wings and fly like...like...like...an eagle.

See?
Trite
Compromised

Fuck temperance!
Fuck temperance!

In her doubled down tippy toes clear water tender reeds and issues
calamitous in the wake of a light you've only ever seen shining from a

demon's ass. Sanity in the balance. Golden eagles or golden showers. One extreme to another see, and who's to say this Even-Steven world won't consume and drown us all? Golden Eagle Golden Showers.
Golden Eagle golden showers.
What am I waiting for? Why isn't THIS the end?
Nothing to be done.
So much more to be done.

It's a game of two halves, Brian, we only gotta stick one in the back of the net and that will give us the advantage. Like one more goal than them. It is not that complicated.

But Temperance,
Temperance; is a fucking work horse, man. Temperance does not rest.
Temperance is a rough Thai massage at best.
Putting me to the test.
At the universe's behest.

"Ať je tvůj život plný dobrodružství."

"Ať máš vždy dobré přátele."

"Ať je tvůj život plný rovnováhy a pokoje."

But until you realise there is no test you will always be a fool.
There is no such thing as a 'foreign' land.

Temperance speaks all languages.
Temperance is mute.
You are its guide.
Don't ever let that knowledge drift away.
You may have lifted the bonds from around your necks, but you are still
 chained to the anxiety of freedom.
As it is above, so it is below.
You will be the last to learn that nature is slow.

Honestly! You have never seen anyone take so long to finish a cup of coffee!
Slowwww.

Animus et Anima.

Krampus or Genome.

In Tremulous Phrases we prostrate ourselves in your presence and pick up your pieces.
In Bibulous Frenzy you Humpty.
In cotton sockses we honour your nudity and ain't so weak we would freak out when we click on your thumbnail and find those beautiful legs are attached to a dude.

"Why go through life with one arm tied behind your back?"
Jim whimpered to the mechanical monkey.
Sincerity is Strength. "Mum, Dad, this is Judy. She's with me."
Women want to be him and men want to be with him.
It is what it is.
Always ask yourself, "How would James Dean do it?"

Barefoot with two big goblets of water, is how. One to purify the soul, one to quench his thirst, and a pool. A pool with dreams in it; and mulch and talking frogs. I ain't gonna kiss it, I'd rather have a talking frog.
That water don't know no gravity. Not on his watch.

Alive again and in real love with a reflection of overweening modesty.
And one foot looks bigger than the other. It's science.
She could be her own brother.
Which one of you's gonna play the plagiarist?

Now you know don't you that when you get back out there, they is all gonna have baggage. You ain't no spring chicken yourself. They gonna have baggage and shit to declare, boyyyyyy.

So, ask yourself twice,
"How would James Dean do it? How would James Dean do it?"

15
THE DEVIL

Laughing like Christians.

They came bumbling into my place all pins and needles and they're looking for a home and I say I'll give you a home but at this stage they are already at my wine and of course I will join them but first I have something I must do.

I lick my multitudinous lips, strap on my accoutrements and drop a postman's sack full of lysergic acid. Strings rising. Strings vibrating. Strings annoying. Strings soothing. Piano rising. Everyone needs a little ol' Me time.

Tarapaca from the Jodo region of synchronicities.
33 bottles each. Check.

They joke around.
"We are the Tarpacas Geddit? The tarot packers….Bwahahahahaa! Like a job see? Packing Tarot cards for a living." Laughing like Baphomet now, the pair of them.

We time.

There is no light blue–hate–free pushme pullyou.
There's a gavel I stole and a nondescript fish and I am all men, money, gods and drag queens. All seens and unseens unclean. Now bleed for me. In dress up. Then FLEX!

When we were six we were clever as clever but you can't stay six forever and ever.
We are not so different you and me, because I AM the true hero and yes, I have a light.

Here, suck on that fiery lolly pop.

We are on earth. Use your heads. Everything is seen. There is nothing to be seen. Back to your hovels, you filthy vegetables. I'll cook you the god darndest macceroni and cheese you ever shat out.
To remain unclean, that is the dream.

And I give you my personal guarantee,
There ain't nobody can sing like me,
Of love,
Of hate,
Of curly fries,
Of sailors.
Even with that plum in your mouth, you are still your own verbal jailers.

No human should ever have to speak 'business english'.
What even is that?

I will twist your words and make you eat them raw. UNLETTERED!

I am tired / I ate my body / I will do it again / and drink too much / and think wrong thoughts / and I will tighten your chains for as long as you choose to stand by my side / and darling…
"Yes hon'"
Your head's not right /

Then the acid hits
"Where did everybody go?" he says to her.
"Where did who go?! Where do you think you are?" she says to him.
"There were people milling around in the kitchen."
"We came home alone," she says to him. "There isn't another soul for miles."

Jan 20th – The most depressing day of the year.

Don't get cocky. Let them bend your ear. Pretend you are listening. They will never suspect a goddamn thing.

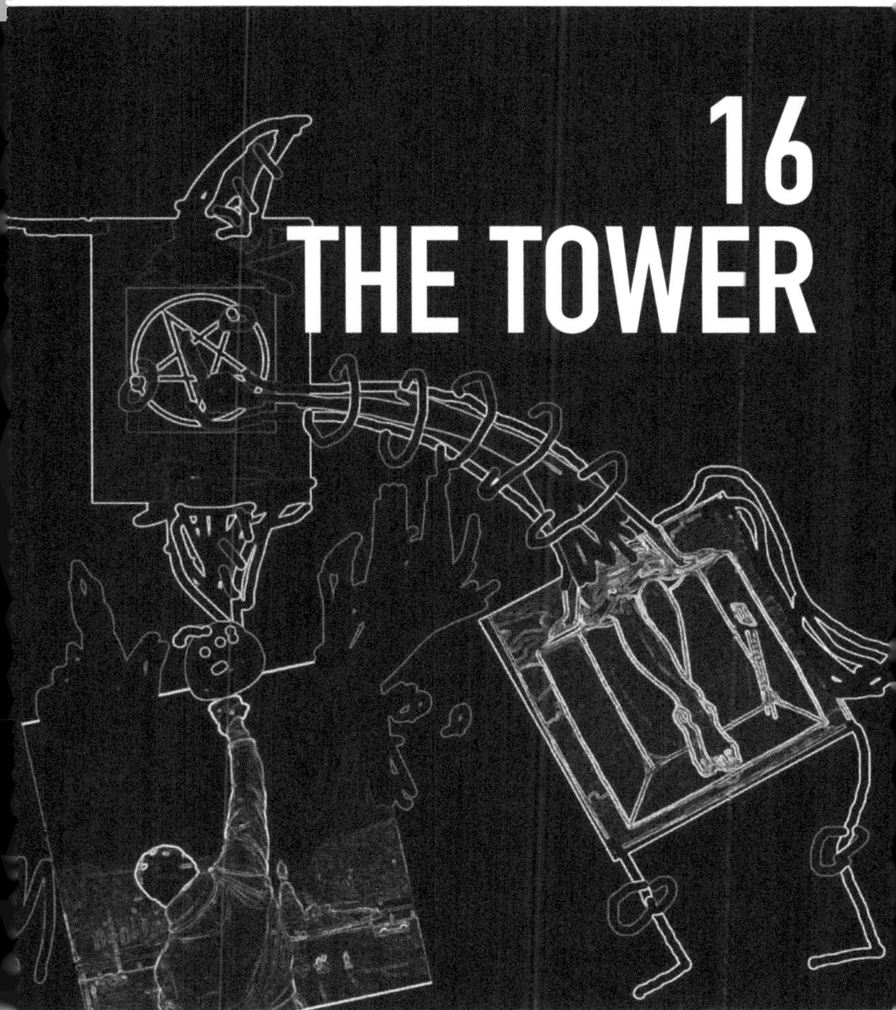

Dear M,

Just gone the witching hour, 12:10.

I knew I would hear from you again.
We make quite the team.
Die Hard & Die Harder.
I have just about had it up to here feeling like a martyr.
But we can look at this two ways. In fact, that in itself is only one way of
looking at it…

What I mean is, I am sorry for kicking you out so early. Man, I am just getting around to kicking the rest of the fools out now! Damn but we had a night.

I'm so proud of us.

I am ashamed.

Shame on us.

I am so proud.

So, we completely trashed my parents home, a job I was never going to accomplish all by myself.

We wanted you there, we really did, but babe–dude, you were only a kid and the things we tried...you would have died.

Get this...some creep called Canada to speak to his girlfriend for two hours. If my parents don't die from a heart attack when they see the phone bill they will kill me twice.

The orgy lasted an eternity. My folks' bedroom is for shit. The living room is a foul pit. The kitchen blaze we decided to leave. The fire department wanted nothing to do with us.

We made Frankenstein babies and fed them acid–dipped jelly tots that cascaded from the sky and I learned to dance on my hands, and nobody wore protection. Can you imagine that? Perhaps you can. You had to be there but...

Anyway, the tower is completely marmalised so you'll have to find somewhere else to stay.

It's funny, when I write to you, everything else goes away.

The TVs were the first things to go, then the microwave, then the dogs, then the dead bodies from inside the walls and the starving children in the basement.

They can't blame me. They made me do it. With their old-time music. Their New Fast Automatic Daffodils. Their penchant for turning a blind eye to the sheer lack of entertainment value in serial killings, ritualistic rape and pets.

In the emptied pool this morning I found words written in fire.

"The answer will come all at once or not at all. Don't you dare cut open that chrysalis till I am done, sir. Only through this struggle will I gain the strength to join you bastards in the real world. I may look like an impris-

oned schmuck now but just let me to my pain and I WILL see you again.
Thrice this size.
A thing that flies.
Dotting all your `I`s."

I had tried to write in god's own tongue so that he could plainly see that our tower of babel was shrunk to the size of a post–orgasmic prick and that one more useless utterance from him would make the universe sick.

I bring them back up.
A monstrous belch.
A screech – Another screech.
A 16-year old's regret at having mistaken her parents for Vogon mouth breathers.

Now ain't that some twist. The parents bursting forth from the grand delusion that was I.

Now, Mum, Dad, listen…
They're playing your song.

"You dancin'?"
"You askin'?"
"I'm askin'"
"I'm dancin'"

…and M, just before I sign off, I just gotta tell ya. I sold my story about the Spread Eagle to The Spread Eagle.

COLM IS FUNNY.
I see the plays that I must bear a part

17
THE STAR

You, you want Greenpeace with a salary. She wants you to take a breath.

Breathe in. Breathe out. And take that small step.
There IS something innocent about morning sex.
She wants you.

Now hear this...
"qoSlIj yItIv!!!" (Pronunciation – Cha ho ta kalla kabrayta) –Klingon for 'Enjoy your birthday'.

I can't believe I can see you. I know you. At this proximity we waited.
Please don't let me finish. Please interrupt.
That language you are speaking. I love that I don't understand you. All of you.
You are the kingdom of Babel naked in my bed. In my chariot. Better. Best. Bested.
In your light I am truth.
I am always pleased to see you.
And I do.
See you.

So that we could sleep, we employed her with her stars, eight–pointed skimming stones playing our song.

In the Tower you spoke gently and with good humour, "You and I would be a disaster."
And although success breathes down our necks, we must (em)brace our-

selves for the imminent revolution. How long before everyone notices that the emperor has no body.
You shone that light in the void and look what you accomplished. Now we can never die.
I am being breathed and breathing.
Conclusions are not friend to the artist.
Our works are footnotes to a most romantic death scene.
An eternal scream.
With tears of love streaming down our cheeks back into the bottomless pool of collective unconsciousness.

And Snoopy was there and Woodstock was there and Ra and Eraserhead and Captain Kirk...
I have the bruises to prove it. Mr Ben style souvenirs of my journey into the unknown where no Liverpudlian has been before...

Mythical constellations.
A pigeon in an Ibis.
A woman in a satellite aloof.
Taurus raised on an enigma.
My mask fallen and the car park bollard sun melted.

X marks the spot.

X

On this stoney ground of twisted rods words are water.
Our love is the... Já nevím co.

It's an okay trick but why you walking ON the water? What are you afraid of?
Breathe in, breathe out and take the plunge. The words will let you in. Just don't try to drink them. There are tiny fishhooks in every syllable. Not to mention the tribbles and mulch.

You let down your guard
And I let down mine
And we squared the circle where the sun don't shine.

You are homeless now and there are no more roads, no vistas of distances and the heat on your neck in window seat No.8 reminds you that yesterday's make up is yesterday's love letter, and what the hell are you doing on a plane?

Get up off your knees.
Listen to the guitarzzzz.
It's hard to make out the lyrics with all that feedback.

But he's saying something about it all being so frustrating. Doesn't matter
though when you play it loud and dance.

I know I will see you again.
I will see you when the ripples of water spell out the name of our first born
and all the artists of the world learn that there is no time between the light
and the movement.
I will see you on the dancefloor.
I will see you where you left me.
Today is a good day but all I want to do is cry.
No chord changes.
No song.
No matter the beauty of the chord.

I will see you on my star.
On even the cheapest celestial map you will find me at the constellation
marked X X X in the shape of a dumbstruck storm trooper.

And remember, to be called a Nimrod is an insult these days.
Remember Babylon.
Remember the fool thought he could reach god by building a tower.
Come to think of it Nimrod was probably an insult back then too!

And but mostly remember, a full artist is an empty artist.
And but
now the broken light can go out.
And but
now the broken fire can be extinguished.

Today the stars appeared because of you
And I lost my house
And I fell in Love.

Breathe now, my red and hidden me.

18
THE MOON

The fear of success draws you back to the tulgy depths of cosmic unconscious, where the trolls of ineptitude wrestle with your luminescence and unfathomable frequencies, paired and unpaired, and frosty to the touch so you look to the black sun beckoning and make believe it will all be okay in the end but the creatures at your shoulder weaken your resolve every time

you stop to think on the immensity of the journey ahead and the infinity of things still left unsaid.

Get outside of your head, it's time all that stuff and nonsense was put to bed. There are no trolls in this landscape to judge your next moves. Go gently into that good night and feel the waters calm and the landscape clear and the howling subside as you scuttle to the fore of your wildest dreams and lay waste to the twin curses of fame and anonymity.

No longer in love with a theoretical phantom but in the thrall of endless possibilities whispering the name of real honest to goodness phantoms. Phantoms dressed in a googleplex of invisible death's head moths.

If in doubt
google 'doubt'.

If in fear
google 'fear'.
If in Dublin
order stout.
If in Prague
order beer.
Don't forget your friends are here.

Don't forget your friends are here and don't tell stories which don't make sense.
You can spend eternity in meditation.
Aeons resting on the Hermits staff.
But where's the sense in loving something if the something you love doesn't make you laugh?

My autocorrect refuses to write the word love without presuming I meant to write live.
My autocorrect ain't just a smarty but has a wealth of wisdom to give…
Don't get caught up in the grammar of emotions.
Listen to your inner guide.
Open your heart let the ocean flood in.
The shallows become the groom, the depths the bride.

Moon tang!

The moon is a sarcasm emoji – is the eye of an Andalusian dog – is the sound round pound found in the underground – is a squared egg – is the o and the o and the o in Donald O'Conner – is fat lady wrestlers in Germany trenches – is the clergyman's sticky wafer – is the hole's hole in the ozone – is Mum up earlier than everybody else to make breakfast and sandwiches to take to school – is the on and off button – is a glorious feeling – is tremulous February – is the end of the line – is a momentary lapse of concentration – is a dark–horse tablet – is Nietzsche's Nautical Necrophiliac – is the required amount of awkward silence – is the Dauphine's snowy vestibule – is Goddess of the blessed cheesemakers – is endless fun – is never the same moon – sometimes licks the back of the sun – has more medals than all the other satellites put together – is a safe distance from good and bad weather – is much bigger in person and is saving up for a hat. A really huge hat.

Who are you texting? What are you watching? Where is your head at? What did you order? Why all the questions? Who's watching Van?
Under the table you don't get the full benefit of the blue moon on the table. But then none of you do anyway if you're all playing on your stupid phones. Why all the judgement? It's not yet time for judgement. Let us be. Don't we look happy? It's you got a stick up your butt about phones. You go figure that out and come back when a friend with a phone doesn't give you palpitations, grandad. You can be such a dolt sometimes. Besides, I'm watching something you just posted, you prick.

19
THE SUN

"You are the King of Wands," she said, "not the King of Wounds," she said she said she said, to him, and it workorked. It worked.

Invalids in designer sunglasses.
Tinted Aqua Marina originals by California dreaming (stroke) Fortuna Bravura horsey ponies.

In
Can
Ta
Tum

Like you just made the cover of a magazine or sold the rights of your book to a publishing company. The world acts you. You still have things to do. A fence to jump, a pal to cuddle, a dance to learn and rehearsals for a play they haven't let you see the script of yet.

You got it right once, big deal.
Now BE the wheel.

Do not turn your strengths against one other.
Absorb and worship the 'sacral' texts.
This is an experience,
Not an idea of one.

This is the Sun, man, THE SUN. Where all religions and beforereligions

began.
The boy is a man.
The woman is too.
Say goodbye to the old songs
And start anew.

You pioneers of a new Aeon.
You may well tremble,
Your task is not light
But you are.
Celebrate your moment of levity.
You have earned it, but beware.
The wall is still there.
At your back and in front of you.
To remind you that you will carry this garden
of Eden with you wherever you
 go. The trick is to let everyone in, let everyone
know.

#notknowingtumblingacrossthelattice

Now sheeeeyyyiiiine!

Exude love. There will be no wall. There will be
no ceiling. There will be pure happiness pour-
ing forth and as you open up, you will see that
the empty space, which you fear may become
a vacuum shall be filled with as much love as
you can take.
A Tolkovsky-sized hug.

The fear that the opposites may cancel each
other out is a game. Opposites belong together. Inside and outside go together. Peaks and
troughs go together. The idea of things going
together and things actually going together go
together.

"What was that you said you said?"
I can smell burned almonds.
"I can smell burned almonds too."

It's February. A mother is meeting a daughter in the library cafe because the husband doesn't want to see the mother. The mother has a bag full of Xmas presents for the children and her daughter. The daughter shows a photograph she has as a screen saver on her phone. Grandchildren.
The wrapped presents she brings out of the plastic shopping bag one by one and then after they are out back, wrapped one by one. To take home. The daughter drinks coffee. The Mother drinks a small Bailey's after her small beer.
The grandchildren must be free from this. The grandchildren cannot know the pain. The grandchildren will receive their presents mindlessly and en-

joy their new toys. The children win but the sun sees all. The darkness in every beautiful moment that defines us all.

"But what if they insist on remaining negative despite all the lessons?"
"Then throw at them all the positive you got."

20
JUDGEMENT

Red

I never put God first.

I've worshipped only false idols.
I've used pretty much all the Bible people's names in vain. Often.
I've worked on a Sunday. A Job in the village in a pub called The Spread Eagle.
I've disrespected my Mum and Dad on countless occasions.
I've not killed people. I've killed things.
I've cheated, stolen, lied.
And I have been jealous of artists, good looking people, my cousin and the rich, and J, who gets more P than I do.
9 sins out of 10.

Brown

I put me first.
I love myself.
I'm proud of my name.
My weekends are pretty lazy.
I don't have kids.
Not suicidal.
I've cheated, stolen and lied to myself for most of my life and occasionally, I am having such a good time that I am jealous of me.

Green

I told a kid in school what I wanted to be when I grew up. Happy, I told him.

You're naive, he said to me. I thought 'naive' was a very clever thing for a child to say. I also thought it was way too cynical for a child to think that way. I wonder if that guy is happy now.

Rouge

The void is behind me.
Surfing the wave of time and space
This,
This has never happened before.
None of it.
We are in the lead.
A cosmic trumpet sounds our victory.
I've been born like this before.
I won't wait for any prize.
I'll play this game in my prime.
Leave regrets to you.
Lay naked with the truth...

I can't do the eye tests
With the little dots.
Red/Brown/Green become one.
I don't know what they mean.
But that doesn't change the colours.
I am colour-blind.
That doesn't change the colours.

Hnědý

I live inside my art.
Not metaphorically like a poet might say but actually inside the art.
It's good.
Comfortable.
I have a mini fridge and a positive mental attitude.
People come and sometimes we take things from the mini fridge to eat or drink.
Not metaphorically,
Like actually come and eat and drink.
I have a long, white, fake fur coat which makes me look like a Yeti. And I have a crazy, white wig that goes really well with it. Not metaphorical clothing. Real clothing.
I know a woman who can levitate. She does this when she comes to my

place. Actually levitates.

Not as a party trick but just when we are talking. Or eating or something.

I am married to my art (actually) so I would never do anything with the levitating lady or even the ones who don't levitate.

Sometimes, inside my art, I play music. Oh, I love music.

I have a badge which reads "Home is where the record player is".

The friends who gave me the badge gave me a record player at the same time. It was for my birthday. Not a real birthday but a symbolic birthday.

I usually have toast and coffee for breakfast, and I walk around the lake on the weekends even when it's raining. Especially when it's raining. Actually raining.

I did that in my white yeti coat and crazy white wig last week and I was trending on YouTube the next day.

One of the not–levitating ones sent the link to me and when she next visited she asked to see the yeti coat.

I didn't show her the real one. I showed her the metaphorical one. Now she can levitate too!

Grun

Your time is up.
You will be alive before dawn.
You will bring others to life.
Stay green.
Stay Happy.
The colours in our eyes don't run.

On our wet and stony path, we should never mistrust fate again.
As rocks will smooth, we will too, we are moulded until we are worn away.

"Frisch weht der Wind
Der Heimat zu,"

The World
surrounds
and enters
you.

"Mein Irisch Kind
Wo weilest du?"

Rojo/סוד/Verde.
Verde/Rojo/סוד.
Your mountains of abstract thought
Housing the secret 8th sin.
Housing Daath & the hero within.

Step outside into dawn's sweet smelling gas stations and stretch your legs
Maybe pick up something to eat and drink. This is the last step of the
journey till you get to your final destination.

It is 3am. Be back at the coach at 3.30.
Any later and we'll just have to pick you up

next lifetime.

BFI
Sight & Sound
CINEMA
OF
PUNK
ART

21
THE WORLD

The World is the only private residential community where its residents may travel without ever leaving home.

Occulus Giftus taming the hawk stealing its 3rd eye and roaming around the pocketguidebookmap of another lion's den. Angel cakes and mad cow patties strewn across the lawn of another Eagle's dawn. The garden out of earshot,
the robot gardener dead of boredom
A nicer word for free love set in stone in place of whoredom.
A Shakespearian minority of word–slingers addled at the benefits of wearing
funny t–shirts, and naked Welsh retreats. Botanically speaking, you're a
flaming faun fanatic. The Age of Reason by her futon spoke of higher things.
And all the good and evil that being open-hearted brings.

One for the money.
Two puts on shows.
Three is the survivor.
Four guides which way the wind blows –
In the happy face of Horus his head stuck out all the windows.

Dada recalls childhood and Didi recalls Gogo.
Life is like a flip–page cartoon carved into a yo–yo.

The 'money' guy trips over his script during number two's dress rehearsal and breaks his leg in sixty-nine places
Number three, the stand in, takes the role and nails it, opening night.
Number four takes out the nails, wraps number one up in the bundle that falls to the stage and sells it to her own sister for the price of a one-way ticket to New York.
And in order to purchase the return flight
Number four's gotta butter up number five, in some timeless, nameless ritual not yet devised.

We all see the mosaic—muse differently, despite wearing the same (cheaper now) VR Goggles. Underwater monsters; demons from the deep; a catalyst for cherubim who protect us in our sleep.
"What would you wear if money were not an object?"
"Money is not an object!"

Goes and it goes and it goes.
Can't stamp a feeling in you.
Not on you.
Not on your bare backside or nowhere.
Won't stick.

Sit back in your cloud cream couch of love and fame.
Lay back in your fluffy red bed of success.
Rest on your laurels and
Savour the fantasy of it all.

One dies, ipso facto none of this is real. If it was real then one wouldn't be able to die! Durrr.

We're talking about liberty, man.

My eyes are heavy. It's been a long game. Don't show me anymore. I can't take it. As soon as you point that light away from me, I am taking a well-earned nap. And when I wake up, you better have left the keys behind and as many torches and swords as I can carry. Fill the fridge and the lake and top up the chariot. Bend the rules, straighten the moon and kiss the playlist hotter. Feed the cat and mend the roads and sack the towers, I want them for my own. To share.
Lubricate the devil's thoughts with golden cups of nectar and pick the star up off her knees. Show her a good time. She always looks so serious. So worried.

Tell her not to worry,
I'll do the rest.
I've got a billion brilliant ideas to put to the test.
But first
Sleep.
You don't even know what it took to get me here. You don't even know. So
judge me not for this midair siesta. I'll dance with you tomorrow. For now.
This is my horizontal dance.

We are speaking for the universe.

Mad laughter. When you see all the lies

At worst, I am a dirty worm of thoughts other people had for me!

Now, the only thing I KNOW is that I know EVERYTHING.

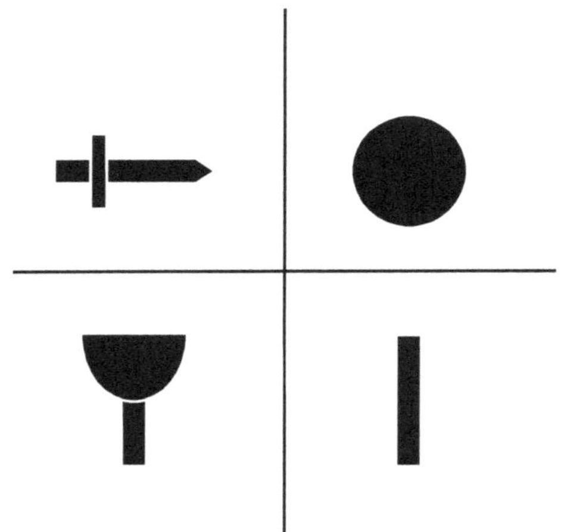

COURT CARDS

Pages

Queens

Kings

Knights

Scary Monsters

PAGE OF WANDS

The happiest Jack, the dancing hack with dreams the size of monsters;
imagination blended with the footnotes to Gerontion.

Nor youth, nor age and a nostalgia for the present,
play to entertain, my friend, or for'er remain a peasant.
The animal inside you, untamed and happy to be so,
and the fool outside a reminder that the abstract swamps you tadpoles
swam were the warmest that you'd ever been.

Catch 'em with a grin because the wand you wield is a delicate paddle
and for every gloop gloop you mumble there'll be three more to take your
place with a pill, a thrust and a whimper. Take that rod and bang one
out, spread your music, bomb the bastards; unleash merry hell and then
describe it till it blushes. Till we all blush. No, we do not know you. You
got the secrets, kid. You got the key. Now make it sound good and give it
to me.

You'd do anything for a little attention, you pretty hyperbole!

A one and a two and nuclear war may be inevitable but until that time
we are going to have a damn good knees up and pray that the King and
Queen can't hear us from their incandescent towers, separated by an infinity of meteor showers, slow hand clapped by the man— made invention
'hours', and in this fiery chaos we can just fuck the symbology of flowers.
Everything is a metaphor for everything else after all. A white rose may as
well be a blue giraffe as long as the Jack of Wands is handing out 'meanings'. Have fun with it, Jack. By the time you get to play the castle, we
might all be stardust again.

You are Mickey in Fantasia, James Dean in The Unlighted Road,. You are a crystal–haired Samson. A princess kissed by a horny toad. Empty your load.

While you still got one to empty.

You are 13.8 billion years old, but you look 20.

Milk it. The Queen's watching...

PAGE OF CUPS

The romantic fool demands of us witchcraft,
of us crocodiles,
of us fishy gods and

Hubble bubble babies wrapped up in the love letters of the merciless Mersey beats and dancing feet at proud and pompous cavern receptions.

I sit alone and think until, until...how does it go?

Waves in a cup, ripples in a daydream, turtles in a sunrise, friends in an
origami lotus flower
...and touch the hand of the future, you who will never let you free.

Cool lesbian mama and zip file Anglophobes bottle the munchkins in a
giant cubs out three-way,
Ogle the necklace, the 32 pearls, mad, obdurate star and promise of a
pomegranate.

4 stages above the waters, the yoni motions homewards, but left to his
devices the homeless grapples remote controls way out of range of the
ships' cable.
With a little imagination we may bring him to his toes, but not without he
shakes off the shackles of illusion in order to make believe for real.
One foot on dry land, two foots in the water,
Could be the son,
Could be the daughter.

....

It's going to be okay, baby.
Alright?
Don't you let go your shield.
Don't you let go your cup.
Don't you believe the hype.
We were all of us born to love.

Lightheaded, slightly shredded, been at the blow since I don't know...
Look! There's a dolphin in my beer!
Don't you text her.
Don't you text him.
Not till you see the ripples on their nipples sip from the brew that is true.

You are divine. Drop the charade. Join the godfish floating in your Gato-
rade before it writes you out of existence.

You are a Jack. You are a valet. You are a page.

Shine. Peel. Rage.

PAGE OF SWORDS

Batfool transforms within the first ring of negativity to an ambition twice the depth of nothing with a speed that belies its intellectual weightlessness.

Bound on a spiralling rack of self-obsession and keen proclamations, I Shall, I Shall, I Shall when I Will is all ye need to know.

The black hole she wishes to fill, with an alter manifest – to breathe, to become a father, a hero, a mum.

The Gods rattled by your insincere costumery, your defensive noise, your hackneyed attackery, your disjointed Freudian quackery.

Should I stay or should I go? Blind faith in your moth–eaten government peeps at you through the mirror of vainglorious misdirection. Choose your battles and self-destruct, mistrust those you pursue, they do not lead.

You isn't little league
You isn't a follower

Youse a representative of stormy issue, all spunk and circumstance. A grovelling ghoul, a tri-partisan transformative. Ghastly unsheathed.
But don't feel ashamed, you couldn't have known you were dressed like a jerk.

So
Summon a thought to beat the wind.
Slash the air into tidier gulps.
Jump over your niece,
Your royalty tease.
One version of you at a time, please.
Stand still, show some flesh, say cheese.
He puts out the flames with relative ease
And mispronounces Betelgeuse.
You got left behind, you ungrabable essence, a dandy under a microscope
Cautious, poised, a Halloween has been,
Tapping on the gate of eternity, the bite size version you know from TV
Tapping to get out, or to gain entry,
You look about you to see which way is forward.

Infinity laughing back at you.

Return the way you came, Adam, and whatever you do, don't drop your weapon.

PAGE OF COINS

"Growing starts when you get tired of your own crap. You are currently hoarding your own crap. Worshipping your own crap.

Advertising it and trying to sell your crap, and, boy, until you realise it's all just crap, you ain't ever gonna be King."

Let's open the date with a little discussion, shall we? A discussion about why we don't fit together as a couple. Maybe then we can move on.

"You are burying your truths to the detriment of your health. You are storing and saving for a bigger, better, brighter day that is already here. Your 'stuff' will go off. You must see that it is you who holds the light and brings the light and gives the light. You are much better off alone. Leave my side.

You do not need me anymore."

But let's have a little discussion about it shall we. Let's see why. Let us get to the bottom of the reasons for our incompatibility. Maybe then we can move on.

"My cards are on the table. I have told you all I can. Our situation is evident to anybody with senses. You are an alter ego, you cannot be yourself, until you drop the belief that your truth will come from being someone else. The court cares very little for you and the only time it gives you, is the time to praise the court that holds you forcefully at arm's length. Read your books, learn the classics by heart and promise to share what you know, but be sure to use the original texts and don't paraphrase for show."

If only we could fathom the purpose of your words. Let us stay a while and contemplate the steps that we must take. Perhaps the answer is in the stars. Hold my hand while we reflect upon the night.

"Away from me child, your enthusiasm tires me. All the planets and suns and comets in the universe cannot guide you. Stand your ground. Earth yourself. Breathe, rest, eat; think of your health. Nought else. Your health. Mental and physical. Stay strong. It is in the present we belong. The moment will release the hero, time shall kill the queen, the King will grow ever fatter as you dance your spirit dance of endless freedom. You are stage manager to the real performance. Your intentions are impeccable. Let's see you step into the limelight, son. I dare you."

....

The moon steers me, and still, I waver;
another's subconscious master of my behaviour.

I am legion yet the message remains unique. Questions hovering about us like a keen, doddery, old librarian looking for a book, breathing down the necks of the happy, settled readers. There is one thing we wish to know and one thing only...

how to be alone with others.

QUEEN OF WANDS

"Every face is unique and lasts a lifetime."

The acceptable is unsanitised.

We must follow every unwritten rule to the letter.

We must conquer the wisdom of the mortals.

The cherries ripen after picking.

The tablet charges after dying.

The self quickens in nature.

Put heat on the lower back and the pain will subside.

Joy is not exclusive to pleasure.

And all the feet and most I would,

I mix the sentence by abiding by

The necessity of motherhood

And the creative grounding of a good, hard scry.

I can make Atlantises out of rat-infested basements with the blurring of a wrist and I can prove men grow on trees and that groundhogs are a thing, and I can turn excrement into gold; not fool's gold but the gold the Atlanteans wrote impossible, lost philosophies with.

There is no distance between me or any moment in the past or the future or the Vltava or the Pyramids or actions and reactions or a big egg.

I can't make you smile for no reason, but I have a million tricks up my sleeve and eight million contacts on my phone and twelve Mars Bars in the boot of my car, and snap and cake, so you know you can trust me, and I don't need anybody's support except when I want it and I know I can get it because, well just look at these legs. I will pop all your cherries, Fisherman

King to flower-scented chicken ladies everywhere.

Your golden gaze.

Feeds me.

Sharpen. Brighten. Contrast. You Like This.

Do I remind you of your mother? Do I remind you of someone else's mother? I can do that. If you want me to. You don't want me to? You DO want me to!

Don't worry, I can be both. At the same time. It's confusing. It's nice. I keep the entire world busy this way and the minute I run out of ideas will be the minute you see the bull that chased your guardian through the Elysian fields of your happiest childhood memories and the lion that ate that guardian whole, and the eagle that lifted your guardian from the belly of that lion. And the Angel at the end who punishes and rewards. Both. At the same time. Until then, wait for a dark-haired assassin's giggling baby ringtone on your next magical mystery train ride to the Krkonoše mountains which came to me by choice and surrounded me and protected me from ever having to open all my eyes.

The Summer feeling extended to a warm hello goodbye. Winter cuddling the rich and the poor with equal fervour and unbalanced results. If I role play your aunts, would that make it easier? Though I thrive in the sun, I am friend to Jack Frost who burns and burns like the best of us and when spring arrives, I will crush your world and I will rebuild it better than you could dream, and if you are very good and behave yourself, I will let you watch.

Marmalade laptops, Maltese Peregrine Falcons, Sabre Toothed Ligers and Cherry Covered Hearses will fall from the Autumn trees into your picnic hamper like loose change falling from the pockets of an underfed juggler, down on his luck, lifted by the raven-haired giantess of the orchard, feet the size of delivery trucks. Little man pegged. Little man pinned. A Vampyr steaked but welcomed in. A bushel and a peck for every typo sin. I may lie and cheat, but I will always win, because I always leave the audience with Atlantean, gold eating grins and the men with erections the size of Africa and the women as wet as the river running through it.

"How early the fruit is falling this season!" Groucho adlibs. They leave it in.

All faces acceptable.

All phases permanent momentarily.

But one song. But one love.

One of each animal. Self-replicating. Both sexes at the same time.

I wear reading glasses in private and sing evenings at the Mandragora cafe.

QUEEN OF CUPS

I met her well,

My Queen of Hearts,
and two years later,

"Goodbye," we said to one another.

For good.

At birth.

Obviously.

For example.

In this way, we live happier than the happiest love birds you ever heard of.

Goodbye
at every tunnel.

"Neboj!"

You are all
Her sisters
and brothers.
She knows more about some things
And less about some things than others.
This is not because she is gifted or dumb
Or because she was born to that Dad or that Mum,
It's because deep within the bowl of this cosmic soup
Rhizomatic perturbances parry,
Not for the glory of winning a point
But for the blessed right to be free
and not marry.
You see, if I knew what you knew and you knew what I knew and the way that
We thought was the same
Poetry and art and comedy and sex
Would be soul destroyingly sane.
So don't laugh if I haven't read Rimbaud
And I won't flinch if you haven't seen Flubber.

Come Closer. Closer. Deeper.

We never miss an opportunity to miss an opportunity.

Those opportunities where your every day love birds would staple a partner's ears to their top and bottom lips and demand fealty in exchange for the staples.

Not us, no sirreee, Bob.

We do not have a 'tender' agenda the way most plebs do.

Tomorrow will not be how we imagined. Ever.

And for every time we say goodbye, we hurt so much we want to die.

When all along, our secret fear is that we might learn to say exactly what the other wants to hear.

And where's the fun in that?

You grabbed my ass and sang to me.

"I'd rather be lonely than happy with somebody new," and you kissed me gently on the neck your, seven brief lessons.

And so, we don't expect too much

Because we don't have to claim to anybody that we are

anything.

Birds do it

And bees do it

wrong.

"Love" is not in a song or in sweet words whispered implausium, ad nauseum

But in this pulchritudinous concurrence of

an extreme case of friendship for which there is no cure

My dear psychic counsellor,

I dreamt of you last night.

You put me up for auction.

And we watched 'The Holy Mountain'.

You relieved yourself all over me

In the shower and we were married.

Our first born we called Solitude

Because a young dog never lies.

I was so comfortable I accidentally spat and spent thirteen straight hours designing red cardboard dresses to put onto animated cocktail sausages for YouTube in the hope that our type of love would go viral.

It's on the cards. It's not on the cards.

The serpents and the sea and you looking over my shoulder at the me you would like me to be, who chirps like a blind horny bishop at my inferior competition but crystallises with you.

We presume the water, and we presume the faith.

As I exit the tunnel now

An angel of perspective.

Who has now absorbed love's powers to manipulate, in order for it to want us to remain

silent.

But One Last Thing First
Out of respect.
Loving with words is living with the dead.
And so
To feel feelings softly
I drink.
To feel feelings dishonestly
I think.

QUEEN OF SWORDS

"The lay of the land, a sniper's view."

Your toes punctuated by nails and literature. Your quill sharpened by Hecubus. You commission the softest, the strongest, the most long–lasting cattle–enabled tumblrs, and only comply with unspoken restrictions.

And you stunned me into silence the hour you laid waste to the Disney–inspired scenery with one stroke of my livid pen.

Motherless all these Aeons, until my struggle to find you consumed my every waking thought, and I began to belong to you more than I belonged to myself.

Secure. Well–fed. I saw nothing wrong with your cold rephrasing of love applied in cotton restraints.

A third party implied by the slant of your sword and the weight of your grimace and the value of your wicked, irresistible impatience.

Kafka floating over your nature complex; riding whilst texting, attending to your footman's needs while ignoring the limited time to attend to this footman's needs.

Don't look at me. I am not here. I made do without you this far. Let's see what Daddy has to say when he gets home and sees the mess you made.

Max Ehrmann, the have–a–go guide who knows your heart by heart.

"Better than love that fails is solitude," the words you are scribbling down there on your handmade paper with floral borders on ripple surfaced beach.

Not for my eyes, but for the eyes of your imaginary friends, (and for the sake of a Poker game for two) Incubus and Succubus, and Beth, Simona and Little Tegal, whose virgin cheeks remember you not. And Cleo whose breasts are strange, and who gives stern love, and fierce with jealousy spends her energy raging at those noiseless dawns, hesitating before joy's open arms, fearing rhapsodic evenings, and a lousy hand, lying awake and set astir by hunger's vow to hold your one good hand and run with you to the end of the misty private runway singing of your hollow, useless being only flight can put right.

You step on me and laugh, then teach me how to laugh. I stomp on Beth and Cleo. If anything, you wax my wroth but in a surge of neo–prolific adoration, I mark down all I do in the portraits that I paint of you.

Pozor PoZar! She is here to cut it short. Her lust for little sausages and semi–naked flames in places hard to navigate without the smacking re(action) of a horny teenage lip at armpit's soul–deep truth.

Pozor PoZar! The wind is changing direction; your sumptuous site and fadeless bloom will freeze that fine erection.

Pozor PoZar! The witch is at it again, the field she ministered by hand she also set ablaze.

The Birth of Elation.

I am stark contrast to day old dread
Or Columbine Winesteins
Or Donald's first wank.
Don't call me Juvenile delinquent
And don't call me 'smoke'
And come to think of it, you better wash your hands and your feet before you
bump elbows with me, you twat!

The written law. A Golem castrated. Kafka undermined and mated. The haters confused at being equally hated. Heaven, we will find, is many gated.

The wedded virgin godmades now sorry that they waited.

You are the one–man trauma mama, artsy, loving, unmuted, but to books much better suited. Your looks a matter of perspective. No, opinion. No, attitude.

A karma trauma seen in a diamond–cut moonstone, crying in front of your great, great ,great, great grandfather's tobacconists. Never apologising. Always thinking. Always the source. Destroying all evidence as sure as Scotch eggs are Scotch eggs.

The Page turned now and ready to do your other side.

Got fourteen eel pie and mash dinners frozen for the future. Fourteen futures.

I stopped the Lynch 'pozar' video at 3:33, which probably means something special. If I were a number, I'd be a thirteen. I despised my elders. Only when I lost my mind, did I become self-aware. The trick, if I may say so myself, is being there.

Thank god I'm not married.

3:33 probably means nothing.

I really

don't

care.

Sigmund Freud and Gertrude Stein

Don their masks and go for wine.

Jung and Woolf trade V.R. goggles.

Their mind jiggles and their body boggles.

And Woolf's final letter to Vanessa Bell, the queen of swords did oversee, with empathy and calculating feminine efficiency, and far less fear for her own end than she had shown for those she loved.

And mother with your back to me and green door tantalising; left ajar –

Inviting me to dig deeper into clouded rooms where once did hide everything that made me shiver, of days to come when you would light the air but only when you were no longer there. A flesh caprice.

The fruit, ripe now, for you to carve. Your forceful isolation welcomed. Your anxiety at having voluntarily self–isolated all these years exonerated.

Now, lightly break up the mash with a fork. Microwave for 5–6 minutes. Stir halfway through and don't forget to fluff up the potato regularly during the cooking time and then if we do get attacked by beings from another planet and the great clown's Star Wars defence system doesn't work, we shall be ready with our pies, pride empowering tides and fluffy, sumptuous potatoes.

QUEEN OF COINS

You'll never walk alone. You don't ever have to walk alone.

Zap! The rocking horse in the antique shop window comes to life. Zap! The toys in the attic begin to play. Zoom! Let's go up the country to some place where we've never been before where Pentacles are Pentacles and tricycles are enchanted and the magic faraway tree belongs to you and me and I will hold you tight, till you fall into the deepest sleep you ever had.

And Fred will be there and Ginger will be there and some photographers from Vogue ,but they want you portrayed all outdoorsy so they'll fly you to Italy and dress you real nice, a metamorphosis, and you'll look the best you ever looked and you are mysterious and ever sought after and the cowgirl boots won't suit you but that is exactly why we will all fall for you and the audience will laugh, but I know you better.

The oxbow sentient, fertile ministry, empires inland, carbon lunged.

I know what you can do with just a little string, cardboard and sticky back plastic.

And if I fell, and if I needed you, and if I were the only boy in the world, and if ifs and ands were pots and pans there'd be no need for preachers, teachers or Ebbets Field bleachers...I...I...I...

And when I arrived at your portcullis steps all destitute and my clothes soaked from the long walk in the rain to get to you, and you rushed me in and dried me off and found clean, fresh clothes for me to wear and sat me down on your big, comfy armchair throne next to the roaring, log fire and brought me hot toddies and toasties and you told me not to hold anything back but to tell you everything and not be shy, and I did and I wasn't and I knew then that there was more to life than requited love and not much more to life than friendship.

And I stayed with you and grew and grew

And now it's hard to fathom

That only twenty weeks ago

You didn't know me from Adam.

And only twenty weeks ago

In that wild, inclement weather

I saw you as my saviour.

My fig leaf-covered Eva.

And when the sun has risen and the yard arm bathes beneath, you will share your homemade nectar and the poems your stepsister left behind of Nietzsche's Nautical Necrophiliac, responsibly out of reach.

She looks like you, but for her twenty-fifth rib, she's never coy in photos and that's how we can tell it's her at the palace press conferences and not you; when you want to go somewhere nice for a walk in the countryside because you just don't have the right energy for a day with the press.

And maybe you wind down at Hot Peppers afterwards and show those ladies how it's done. I mean, you never forget your roots, even when you're the world's greatest Mum.

Now all five senses tingle; the four elements commanded by industrious spirits; your bare arms and bare legs and your bald, pointy cone head making you one of the most conspicuous strippers ever to rise from Malkuth, leap higher than Assiah.

Rung by rung,

From dirt to diamond,

From root to crown.

A killer rabbit mentions you in its kill manifesto, mistaking your boat race for a carrot.

Ovid missed that one and was exiled to the Black Sea for the lost poem and one mistake.

And I wake from my power nap, in your strong arms feeling brighter and smarter, more hard working and with a much better dress sense. While it's making me feel so good, can I stay here? I promise not to be too loud, and I won't ask too many questions, and I'll bring you breakfast, which I will hunt myself, and I don't see a ring on that finger, are you back in the market or did you leave your ring in the club?

I can go and fetch it if you need it. Will you be okay alone? You look like you will be okay alone. I'll leave you alone. That's enough listening for one day.

Thank you.

Let me let you sleep now.

Let me let you sleep.

Goo'night, sweet lady.

Goo'night.

KING OF WANDS

How did I even get here? Like I just woke up and was sitting here with all these trees around me and a half full ash tray and these empty beer bottles.

All this and so little effort.

And this getup. No armour. Secure in my own skin.
The ease of everything...
Safe in the text. Caught in a thought. Another's thought? GoD forbid.
These are my notes.
Are they? I forget. How I love to forget.

The Grandeur of Delusions. We are all alone. There is no one to turn to.
Not my friend. Not my wife. Not my children. Not my books.
I've been lusting after a ghost orchid, but there are no ghost orchids in this forest and so I write about them so I can read about them to my friend and my wife and my children.

"Plants have no memory."
Plants have no memory.
If we quote small enough, can we call it our own?

So, there's this one plant. You would love her. She was everything to me. I thought I meant everything to her but that didn't turn out to be the case. She loves everybody see, and I was just a stop off. She left me sitting here on the porch happy till the happy wore off and wondering how I could become as big hearted as her.
And it happened. I think it happened.
After all, I got a wonderful friend and a beautiful wife and great kids and

all of these trees that surround me now. And his book that I am holding like a lover – the one I keep forgetting.

My deus ex machina.

Those woollen greens, the Kings before me, branches like flames, entrails, rhizomes, theories, explications, umbilical cords, extra sensory perception, the brilliance that emanates from the marionettes' perfectly formed 10 fingers and 10 toes like swords into the cosmos, a light for this new Aeon, a prayer for this new GoD sitting here, ass aching, waiting for something that hasn't presented itself yet but is bound to appear sooner or later, If I can just keep my head, stay warm, stoke the fire burning inside.

I have proved myself
And my love
Cannot die.
Not as long as I remain
Master of my craft.

KING OF CUPS

Art beauty subconscious therapist.
Fickle.
Egoless.

There's a long way to go to become the king when you are already the King.
And I know what you're thinking, but I don't know what I'm thinking.
You're thinking you know what I'm thinking.
No. It's not that...

A name I am stepping on, light and drier and fear has been cut from my cortex and you tilt me forward, and the bit of my brain that is left tells me to throw my front legs forward to stop me from falling from your fingers. It's nature. Not my nature. Nature's nature.

Sometimes I pretend to be you and I, out on solid platinum wig and the toes you sucked now diamond studded know–it–alls, which I wouldn't trade for all the T in intertextuality.

There is more to the air that we breathe than meets the I.

We got to get together sooner or later and the only way you gonna do it, princess, is by placing a big wet kiss on this amphibian's bouche.
Your amuse gueule pre conjugal finger jam,
I'll join you when a man I am.

Did Beckett hang the fool or did the fool kick the Beckett? You can bet your sweet Vltava flowing that he didn't see you coming! No, a smile is not enough, and neither is your meek philosophical keepsakes, not for this gigantic heart, not for this empower rat, not for this I sold my books and put faith in the four-pronged pillow of my night mask.

You missed me once and turned this mouse into a rat. Now find your centre, stroke it softly and count your tit graves; there ought to be an accountable accountant for that. Here he is, here he is, hiding under my horny toad cladding, my erstwhile avatar, my turnabout road mummy wrapped in yesterday's bloody bandages.

And calm and calm, you are calm now you came. And calm and calm, you are calm now the subconscious has been given a name. Subconscious. That's it. Says nothing but...subconscious. Isn't even called that when it's French.

Subconscient. All the T. The difference it makes to me.

PodvedoMí.

If I wasn't such a horny toad, your rocking might lull me to sleep, but you, my Queen, you have struck me where it matters.
Deep in my underthoughts.
My unlife.

A miniature pack of cards forced far under the red nail of your curling ring finger.
I kiss it but it doesn't work that way round.
A puckered life of misrepresented exasperate. The gas, oil and multitudinous lubricants applied to keep me alive until I can connect with the roots of a universal love in the palm of your hand. Royal T. Divine Tav.

The end was set from the beginning. The completion of truth. The restoration of all of existence in the goddess' deafening orgasm. Settled till you swap hands and I am brought to life once more. Once more the recurring sign, the oneness of the Aleph wrapped neatly and labelled....mine.

KING OF SWORDS

Bring on the rain, I will wade through your floods and take down the physical elements one by one till infinity and I are done.

Trap erasing, alligator keys blackened and whitened and the peddles long lost beneath the sweat of your furrowed brow; a daguerreotype of our favourite flavours underscored with a chalky insouciance rivalled only by the friendship bracelet keeps you from suffocating in the belly of your own mind Sylphs.

The praise of the intellectual is the praise of folly but see how happy it makes us to look at and into the rear end of our behaviour and legitimise ourselves with symbols. Spirits of hope dotted about the sky; mythological beasts in the firmament; ego-driven chariots ridden through the stars by imaginary coachmen, dead of exhaustion and ready for their crown and their sceptre and their nice cup of tea.

One glyph, two glyph, three glyph, four...

Perhaps universal karma will come with just...one...more...

A cold, bold approach to the automaton autonomania; it don't matter how many lines you scratch into my naked back, I still ain't gonna push play till you materialise with that cup of tea I asked for and maybe one of those little cakes you mentioned you bought today. Even intellectuals need cake.

The cake in the shape of a cog, and 10 candles sprouting from the central axis of Saturnalian debris fallen from white, empty nothingness. You gotta laugh. I mean what you gonna do when you do have all your cakes AND eat them? Fuck the cakes? There is no fear of us thinking ourselves to death, but we may cause the destruction of an empire ignoring the bond between thought and action and the all-important love in between.

It ain't a watery grave we's wading in, it's desire.

7 yods, me in two, all in one.

Pull up and, from a great height, the charioteer amongst sister stars sees all there is to see; the hermit, the magician, the one in the eight, the seven in the three.
One apostrophe standing alone, unable to shift without heirs to the throne.
One quotation mark seeks mate, ideally leading to romance, love and future double dates.

One thought to bind them all,
And one more thought to sink them.

A robot butterfly engraved on the ring of his Saturn finger.
A clockwork birthday cake in the shape of the planet earth.
Gemini man, boneless doppelgänger.
I'd hang up me hat but I'm missing a hanger.

KING OF COINS

The cycle stopped, your ship a tattoo, no more roving for you

HIT THE DECK!

A Trojan horse in a woman's skin.
Argonauts softened.
The ABCD of corpses in her mouth.

The luxury of an in–house soothsayer masquerading as telephone sex masquerading as a philosophy of chastity and a safe passage through.
Lulled into that secure sense of falsity.

That was the old you.
Best burgers in Prague they say.
Your idea of luxury?
A solid gold cloud and a heart as big as a wrestler.

"You've done us proud – Have a biscuit."

Keeping it tight despite your penchant for indolence calmly counting your peccadilloes as you preen your adventurous past. Your act of compensatory factor a solid gold mast.
Peg it! Leg it! Smug it!
I will look good lying in repose.

"Kiss my hardy."
Wit...damn...there go the pips!

Vena Cava arm.
Arteries for lips.
I got sixty kisses in a mermaid's purse and ventricles for hips.
My hair is veiny, my aorta is brainy.
My atrium is full of water, she's young enough to be your granddaughter!

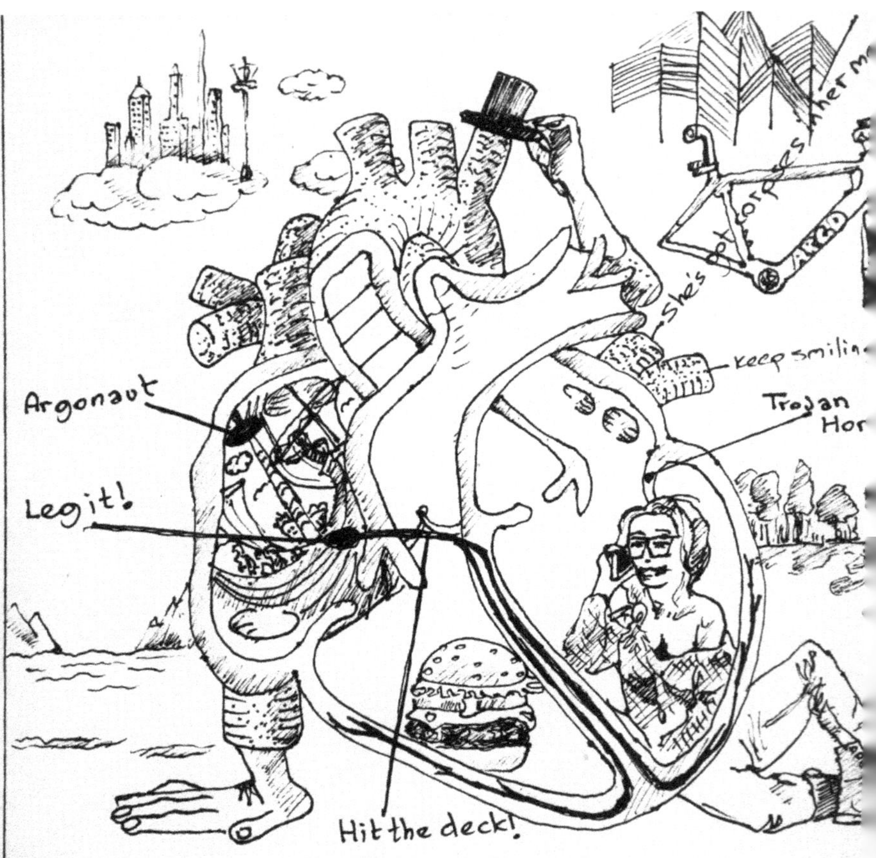

You are the best of us, and you are the worst of us.
I want to be you. I don't want to be with you.
You are a liar.

Only in the clouds of the ace up your sleeve do you dare even dream of such excesses.
Your age will match your lucky number and you will cop on, brother. You is not magic itself.
You step back from your own mind to understand all things and all things stay out and look on you and declare WAR and PEACE and the third thing.

Phase 13 in which Dorothy gets her votes.
"And by the way, I am his granddaughter, and he is steady, he is reliable, he is old," she says of him.
"He's a dote," she says.
"All downhill from here," she says.

KNIGHT OF WANDS

Double me.

Double you. Upside down. Alternative tentacles. Snow scarred. Madness app. An app for madness. Imagine. An app just for loonies with nothing better to do but dance on ice with stars that aren't there to see you to see you nice.

Damn you Mickey. We'll all be gone soon! What we gonna do. "Enjoy it."

My mind is spotty.
The lake is scratched.

Mickey, dude, I don't dig art which is based on pissy fads and soluble news items. Far more interested in the BIG picture. You get caught up in the scritchy details, current affairs and fashion, and you are fucked to begin with. Mick, man, The Fool is there to make the big scary decisions. The Knight of Pentacles to make them work. What am I here for?"

"To not do anything unless it gives you a sexual thrill."

No conflict, no poetry.

No fad but permanent revolution permanently.

Stop kidding yourself. An uneventful podcast would destroy you. You were born to be reborn.
The attention span of a salamander, the sex drive of a Shaw's Jird, the kick of a mule and the attention span of a salamander.

The answer 42. Yiiiiiiiisss. And ears for wings. Wing nut head catching all the thoughts in the kingdom. Eyes peeled for porn and breakfast. Eagles fucking lions till sexuality becomes enriching spring and you are free once more to do your thing!
Clean dirt. Turned on by purity.
Torn between clarity and beautiful obscurity.

Cavaliers bragging about who paid the most for their ride and what's even the difference between being average or great at something that is going to be burnt in the fire of a million Suns come the end of time?

"And what even time is it even?"

"Time is a manmade construct. There is no past or future or present as we understand it, but an infinite, borderless bubble of nothingness separating itself from itself by means of an impossible logic designed by nobody for nobody."

"Yeah, but Mum says I have to be home for tea by five."

Do what you will.
Will what you do.
Logic dictates, senses rebel.
Our intellect dictates that feelings are the way to go.
Our feelings never dictate,
they show.

Time to Show. Not tell.

KNIGHT OF CUPS

Walking in the rain in the back of a taxi.

Hailing a cab from the haven of a bed
Jilted and strengthened.
Welcomed and strengthened.
Heart tattooed with tramlines.
With me as a member.

In the star park, I met Betty Grable. I had to look her up. Seen her in old Black and Whites, How to Marry a Millionaire and Mother Wore Tights. The pin–up girl of my fantasies, right there, in the star park. I was not shy. I had been preparing for this surprise my whole life. And now that I was twenty-one, I was not going to screw it up.

Running behind the one camel, which was wearing a King,
Hiding behind the mouse with a satchel full of coins.
Sharing but jealous.
Covetous but haloed.
Brain addled by rumours self–perpetuated.
"If she figures this one out, she's good."

"You put a diamond in my horseshoe. I woke up screaming. They hung you up in Hollywood boulevard, outside every non–stop diner, outside every unpoliced gas station, every unpeopled five and dime. I had to protect you, so I rushed you back to my room. There we played cat and rat till the cows came home. Or I played cat and rat with the cows till you came home, I can't quite recall. Didn't you play with Lauren Bacall? What was she like? No, never mind, it's you I love. There I said it, I love you. Everything about you reminds me of you. Except you!"

Tearing at the laundry now it's clean enough to ruin.
Melting in the snow, angry as a shepherd.

Cold but happy.

Hot but happy.

Guts trampled by cherubs in the light drizzle of a lazy autumn afternoon
...in your pyjamas.

Most art is a distraction. It has woken nobody.

My first fetish – cards. My first hate – card games.
There was something better for a pack of cards to do.

Collecting cards. Star Wars cards, Vampire cards, Monster cards. The feel
of the pack in the hand (a precursor to the portable phone).
Cosy, snug, full of life and infinite possibilities. Chance and beauty which
you can put in your pocket.

Begbie : Did you bring the cards?

Sick Boy : What?

Begbie : The cards, the last thing I told you was to mind the cards!

Sick Boy : Well, I've not brought them.

Begbie : It's fucking boring after a while without the cards.

Sick Boy : I'm sorry.

Begbie : Bit fucking late, like.

Sick Boy : Why didn't *you* bring them?

Begbie : 'CAUSE I FUCKING TOLD YOU TO BRING THEM, YOU DOSS CUNT!

Sick Boy : ...Christ.

KNIGHT OF SWORDS

**You got me nervous.
Watcha do it for the puppets for?
You a Hero for nuthin'.**

Take off your mask.
You're just a kid.
A kid.

You want to impress the ladies?
Show your process.
What do you see?
I know you look ahead.
Ditch the 'cool' act.
We are all hermits, but you.
You...

Pull up your hoodie.
Be a goodie.
You got the Princess and the Queen in your thrall.
Enjoy yourself.
In terms of movies you could be an opener.
Stay aggressive.
Your day will come.

You got a gun.
You got a gun.
A girl and a girl and a gun and a gun.
Don't show it unless you're gonna use it, blue.
Don't worry so much if you don't know what to do.

You got a gun.
You got a gun.
You'll muddle through.
Besides,

BLOODSTAINED | Urban
THE MAKING OF
RECYCLE

Those goggle-eyed ladies have got your back.
Let them 'feel' for you.
Let them 'intuit' for you.

Grab those reins of logic and steer yourself to utopia.
Whether or not there will be anyone there waiting for you matters not
As long as you can talk your way into existence.
Power is a great disguise.
Those in line for the thrown.
This they have long known.

Fuck those guys.
Bury your hoodie.
Trash the mask.
Saddle up and say who you are.

KNIGHT OF COINS

The trepid explorer.
A sensitive killer. Slows down the bad guys with an old tale of the new world order.

Dullifies their mental bootstraps while magnifying their weaknesses, then swoops like a Valkyrie, topless, pimped and kinky. Quietly so.
"You ever seen your arse in the mirror?"
No, you smooth talker, I ain't.
"Well, it's good."
That's all he has to say and all he needsta.
Mummy's boy, flattened butterfly, our tears outlined then hid in Thalia–mascara Templar templar, easy does it, don't lose your rag over no flying fuck at a rolling donut, there's money to be had if we just hold it together and dress for rain.

In a bubble but very well read, keeps his horse and mind well fed,
Never says anything unless it needs to be said
You gang up and cross him, he'll make you dead.

Violent.
Silent.
Always wears a rubber.
Adorable attachment to a long-forgotten lover.
Garda with a bully club.
Milk and Pickles.
Doesn't like tickles.
Aims his insults fair and true so they help you much more than they could ever hurt you.
Clever that way,

And forty percent gay.

PIP

Wands

P

Cups

CA

Swords

RD

S

Coins

WANDS

I
ACE OF WANDS

Aux premiers rayons du soleil.

"Duck!"
Thank you for being a friend.
"Duck!"
Thank you for the music.
"Duck!"
Thank you for not explaining everything to me like I'm a child.
"Here. For you. Take it.
Fetch!"

Thank you for leaving the answers but for forgetting to let us know what the question was and for giving us something which was not an answer but was a birthday gift and here we are asking the price. You must think us so rude, but we will find out the price anyways because, if I am not mistaken, most of us here are planning to take the gift back to the shop from whence it came and get a refund in the hope that the cash back will give us more pleasure than this weird choice of present, which I suspect is something you wanted more than something that you thought we wanted. Anyway, thanks for trying, but frankly I think I can do better and god knows I am going to try.

JUSTWATCHMEGO!

Don't take away all this potential before I have figured out for myself that, sure the young oughta be sued for breech of promise, but please don't take away all the days of fun, yes fun, that I intend to have ignoring the obvious and chasing after the dream of 'the obvious'. The dream of what's happening to me is so much more attractive than what's actually happening to me. Until I realise all by myself that I have been chasing my tail, trying to grab my own fist, trying to jump over my knees, just let me be. Don't be judgey. In my heart, I know you don't even think about being judgey but my mind tells me you do and it's peace of mind that I am not ready for; not with the fire that's in me now. Let me burn and shine and light up this shithole, at least try to make it look liveable-innable to the masses who don't think as much as I do; to those fools who just…live.

"DUCK!"

I am all Sephira.
I am all Paths.
I was twenty-one years when I wrote this song.
Now I'm twenty-two.

"FETCH!"

We are the source of creation.
We are yet to come into existence.
We are none and we are two.

Kether.
Ether.
The the.

I ain't no soul miner and I ain't your dog.
I have a large pair of gonads.
We're all of us monads.
Absent Dads.
Fucking Fantastic Fads.
I am not for sale, but I love making ads.
If you cannot make goods from bads,
You ain't never gonna be one of the lads.

Duck yerself, brother! I am 4 Real.

"And now it be's a scary fish!"

NEW YORK
CITY
ordinary cleaners
reach only this far!
candy

II
TWO OF WANDS

2.22pm
We made our connection.

You drank down my tears. I wept for my success.
You cut the head off Orion to seal our inter–stellar blood pact.
The flutes pointed at our funny bones. "All battles should sound so sweet,"
you sang, and I smiled at you smile.
But beyond the battlements of your vigilance, I saw no ships.

3.33pm (workout/shower)
Meissa in my grasp. Your beauty tethered to Betelgeuse and Bellatrix.
Oh, you shining one, cloaked in black light. I delight in the challenge you
present. Your thoughts well met. My sight recovered in your sight. Your
Joycean colloquialisms spilled like alcohol offerings to dead gang mem-
bers. No rumble regretted. NO sentence of mine unvetted.

4.44pm
Shopping list – Roman candles / Diet epiphanies / Divine–intervention
Flakes and Mother's mawkish milk.
Your lucky number holding dominion over our royal hangovers. My lucky
number submitting to the balance you offer in your own entrancing version of the Mississippi Delta Blues and television adaptations of your favourite dress.
I dreamed I was the ten of cups; freed from all covidiots. Rapturous ap-
plause from the windows of the apartments in the street. Happy families
showing them how it's done.
Kierkegaard's knight of faith cantering through the light traffic, helmet
closed, knickerbockers flapping in the wind, his bold steed weaving in and
out the puddles of your Joycean covidioms.

5.55pm
Little willow, dancing like a dreaming puppy, fate smiles on you, you read
your own thoughts well.
But now you must translate them into a larger living language / giant–
speak / Kraken–talk.
God–smacked, 5 loaves, Jesus–Christ–Reduced, clean your house, purify
your passion. She's well-groomed even when she doesn't have to leave
the flat and the statistics she hangs on her walls like trustworthy lead-
ers, promise an acid free, non–toxic, light fast, photo–safe archive of soul-
ful penury to laugh at when we look back from our own seventy-eight
stallions, remembering all the time to stay in character until words form
themselves and we are free to paddle in their cooling fluidity.

The man walking on the headland looks out of perspective. Either he's a
giant or it's salt sea air 'special' perspective or we are looking at him wrong
– See! He must be quarter of a mile away and he's the same size as the kids
playing in the sand there. What's his deal, man?
"Although infinitesimal, my position two metres to the left of you renders
me unqualified to comment without skewing your conjectures and hy-
potheses. But yes, he does look weirdly big."

6.66pm

And now with paper in my hand I'm beginning to start to think I might understand that the journey is longer and darker and harder in real life. Who knew!

Six–Threlty: I'm not saying my mother–in–law's fat but…

Stop right there!

It's the salt sea air. It acts like a magnifying glass. That man looks bigger because there's fire in the water, man. There's fire in the rain. There's fire in the mist and the dew. Over to you.

I'm not saying my mother–in–law's fat…no, wait. I am. She's fat. It's not her fault. It's glandular from anyone's perspective.

She hasn't yet tried everything.

Now the world is young.

Sell me that globus bar.

If I screw up my eyes and move in uncomfortably close I can probably pull one or two humans off this rock and make some valuable comparisons under a microscope. The small made big – the recurring dream feel of the pinhole camera in a black hole heart.

There's fire in tears. Everything is exaggerated.

I put this down to mirrors.

III
THREE OF WANDS

In the playzone — bursting apart — A gestation scythe — An invasion gimp — The cowgirl herd and herder absolved of third-degree murder.

"I'm truly sorry. I only ever meant to hurt you."

The seductress swallows – The U.F.O. unopened – The cannibal who sires inedible children – The combobulated energy of a blaze saint.

"You don't need to apologise to me if you don't like Tom Hanks, you just need to take a good long hard look at yourself!"

A hooded turtle. Mother Superior's game face. Raindrops on your legs. The capsule wreckage reading 'Ouroboros! Your country needs you!'

I tend to get overexcited at the sight of a Beatles mop top or a good old fashioned Catherine wheel spewing sparks of light back into the black of Ringo's Arthurian satellites.

"Triangle Man?"
"Yes."
"Triangle Man, what's the opposite of tea?"
"Coffee."
"What's the opposite of dog?"
"Cat."

EDS You
G'NIGHT
White Trade
123
CHAIR
OPPOSITE

"What the opposite of mouse?"
"Pineapple."
There can be no opposites without the third point defined by its relation
to two others. No measurable distance without three.
"Triangle man?"
"Yes."
"What's the opposite of infinity?"

I am the lord of established strength. I am the hermit as a young man. I
am the reflection of the moon on the water. I am the busty Bohemian (N)
un (13)
Harm meant.
Harm done.

The nameless will win.

Atziluth!

Bless you.
Thank you.
Don't thank me or the devil re–enters your body!
I don't mind. Where did you hear that anyway? The devil re–enters your
body!
I don't know. I can't say nothing though. It would be rude. I can't just say
nothing.

Atziluth!

One minute's silence.

Now never mind the wheres or whys, just hold me tight. I've got an idea
forming which will affect us all. Hold me. Hold me tighter. I'm close baby.
I'm really close. Don't let go. Don't ever let go. I know, I know, I know, I
don't belong here.
But we are safe from harm.
And I love you with all my art

IIII
FOUR OF WANDS

When this is all over and we can all go out for a walk again, I am going to perform a ritual in the forest.

When all this is over and we can go out for a walk again, I am going to
train myself to enjoy the forest while I am performing a ritual in it.
When all this is over I am going to teach myself not to regret that I didn't
make a ritual of enjoying the prison in which they tamed us. Four walls,
a fire in each quarter, trees she bought and attended and laughed and
siphoned the court through the fingertips of bellicose, jade mushroom
glands.
Uploaded but buffering, saved but closed to callers of an age where temperance flies in the face of utilities unboiled to brusque methods, too early
to tell yet if the waters will come between us or carry us through the
branches to a fridge stuffed with renal reckoning.
The prince is sick too now and won't ask for help.

In the forest, during the ritual, we will get that son of a bitch to stand
guard and he will piss his pants waiting in the dark for our nocturnal news
reports about serendipitous messages sent at the same instant between
government marionettes and famous Czech actors looking out for the
people with songs of patience and love.
If I held you in my arms do you think it would help you remember what
numbers came up in our future. The reading quickening as the deck shuf-
fles itself in the starry firmament of our warm coffee breaks and wild
equinoxes.

"Next level stuff," she said as we packed for the woods and made hay while
the trains were empty. Slowliness, a crime in these world–weary times;
I would be the queer visitor, the rag tailed traveller you invite into your
home and feed with an abundance of sugar–coated jury magnets. I bring
myself to your judgement, so it doesn't count.

When this is all over and we can go out for a walk again, I will walk by
your side, and you will walk by mine and I will not walk faster, and I will
not walk behind you and you will be within reach, and it doesn't matter if
you are to my right or to my left, although the left might mean something.
Left and right probably mean something but it depends which side you
are looking at us from, so in that case, there is no left and right. Not at the
same time anyway.

An artist's work is never done.

You are a cucumber; a cabbage and you would have been king if that
tripe had any bearing on our current abstract mathematics. Your thorn
of crowns is off trend and your Guru rots like the best and the worst of

them, exoterically.
Anyroadup, we have crossed the city boundaries and we march purposefully to our as yet unmanifested rewards.

A celebration gif made good and liked in the hands of two copulating lady
mirages and the four stone statues impossibly wrought by the ancestors of
a legendary giantess. Easter eggs hid in the gates of the wolverine scratch-
es of the conceptual floral rangers, Mod–clad.

It's summer and the smells of the afternoon meal rise to the bathroom.
The shower is cool, and the day was long. The wine is opened, and the beer
is chilled. The fish has been gutted and the meats marinated. This evening
will be an evening to remember. I will go down before they call me to join
them. I don't want to miss any of this. I am beginning to understand. I
love it when I feel like this, and I wish I could feel like this forever and I
will never even really know what it is to feel what I am feeling until I can
do it without worrying about the imminent loss of the more than affable
aforementioned aftermaths.
When this is all over and we can sing again and show off and talk of
things other than the awful situation we are in, we will go to the forest
and perform a ritual.

First – I will fashion a small wooden boat out of the bark of a beech.
Second – I will gather a basketful of acorns and choose the greenest fullest
forms to pretend–man the vessel.
Third – I will paint the boat and name the players, and the boat, and I will
attach an oil–soaked sail to its mast.
Fourth – I will line the hull of the boat with the only copy of my 1000-
page manuscript.
Fifth – I will light the sail with a match taken from the handle of my
Rambo knife and launch the boat into the stream.

As the boat burns all brown and green and wordy, I will sing what few
sentences I can remember by heart from the manuscript until I run out of
memories and am left with nothing but the breeze and the half bottle of
wine we kept from the lovely train journey.

An artist's work is easily done.

Come on, turn those smiles upside down. 8 billion unexplained bridges.
Four Pooh sticks. Belonged to Benvolio, before he forgot to mind his
ownio, and with well–meant encouragement lead us all to our untimely

completion.

The anti-party preceded the proviso that the first must be last and the playlist must swing and the stripper was the succulent anchovy on the trod–upon cake.

An artist's work is easily undone.

Viens à nous. Tu es invité. Viens comme tu es. Apporte du Toblerone. Nous adorons le Toblerone. Une grosse barre ! Le chocolat qui ressemble à des pyramides. Nous ne retiendrons rien, nous ne nous retiendrons pas, si tu ne retiens rien, si tu ne te retiens pas. Nous te montrerons comment être libre. Nous te montrerons comment te retrouver. Si tu nous apportes une grosse barre de Toblerone. N'oublie pas le Toblerone.

And when the ritual is all over and we walk away…

FIVE OF WANDS

Striking poses. Licking cans. Catching hell from the man.

Let me get my hands on the gormless fucker; wipe that shit-kicking grin off his greasy lips.
Behind Nana's cinema screen in silhouette, we can see her (hourglass figure turned upside down and running) ask him, "What will the gang jacket read?" He picks her up like heroes do and carries her off to the black limousine parked out back.

"Thunderbirds," he says, "We are called the Thunderbirds."
With heads in hands, we call upon our spirit animal to walk us safely across the zebra crossing and feed us milk duds as we learn how to do it all by ourselves. My chain dangling free and skipping behind me till we get to the tree trunk, which I would always climb up then jump from, shouting, "GERONIMOOOO!"

I cry when I think of you, now you are so far away. Locked down here with nothing but my memories and my television. "Did you hear what the buffoon

HYBRIT
LIDE SE
BOUŘÍ
بربري
T
BIRDS
RIOT
Ευδοκῆ ἢ μὴ ὑπάρχη ὁ λόγος
ton visage

said on the news last night?"

Compassion will out. Leave him to his bed of nails and lack of anything resembling intelligence. Tu devrais voir ton visage. Tu as l'air d'un imbécile.

The chemical table weighing in on the matter with heavy hands and penile dysfunctions and, oh boy, if you think these teenage delinquents will let that go by unnoticed then you were born under a powerful mean star.
Push push push.
Hold me back. Hold me back.
Push push.
Hold me.

And don't hit my lightsaber too hard. It's only thin plastic. Just lightly like that. I know it's not the same but that star spangled twat wouldn't give us anything sturdier than the promise of a fucking miracle.

We'll be ready for the call up, sister, man, brother.

"You know what Mum said to me yesterday after I told her I'd been to the army recruitment centre, and they told me I could be sent abroad within a few weeks and be a sniper? She looked at me sadly and said, 'You're not a sniper, Carl.'"

The great temptation is to pulverise him, but I would settle for punching him in the eye. Transsexuals and transvestites and the binary males and females and asexuals, pansexuals, genderqueer, non-binaries, the questioning and heterosexuals and the wholly disinterested shall rise and the harmful and tragic news will be heard throughout the known unknowns and the pope, and the devil will hold hands and dance an awkward dance like Harry and Hermione did in the tent in film of the book Harry Potter and the Deathly Hallows.

We shall surpass labels until our alphabetti spaghetti runs deeper than Woden's letterbox.
Teach me all your best karate moves and krav maga and I promise I'll give you the best goddamn foot massages when all this is over.
Who needs the peace corps when you got Fred and Ginger rioting like pixelated Martians in the brown cleavage of Picasso's youngest mistress in the arms of the hero in the back of the limousine?

"Dobří Lidé Se Bouří. Good People Riot. That's what it reads on my jacket. It's not a gang jacket like yours but it's instigatory, don't you think?"

I do. Now take it off.

The spotlight drifts from the ace bunch with their big sticks to the storm
drains of Venice, California, where a normal sized man with a stick of his
own is zooming around in a child's red pussy wagon. His purpose? To ex-
plode the idiot president with nuclear powered satire and 'tiny little dick'
jokes. Oh, and rip the concrete heart from his spindly, rotten chest. Then
run over it with his pussy wagon.

No conflict, no poetry. No movement, no strife.
No guns, no grenades, no throwing stars, no knives.
Just sticks at this stick party. And cider. Lots of cider.
And the dancing girls of all elements.

SIX OF WANDS

I got a medal and loads of accolades and a gold cup and important people said nice things about me and I was feeling tip top and

then, as if nature had been jealous of my success this whole time, the capricious siren nudged in like a prick with tattoos and a scruffy beard in a supermarket queue and started killing all the humans.

And now, all the fun stuff and the philosophical stuff and the political stuff means sweet F.A.!

Too little charity too late.
Too much hot air too long.
Too many baddies ignored too well.
Too few days off or orgies.
Too
Many
Sun.

Too bad we never did this and always did that and should have said this and coulda made much better music together if we had only understood that this would not last.

Our painted facades coughed and our stripmined insides boiled and the system we had set up for ourselves suddenly seen for what it is, a gigantic farce to one and all.

But still, I have my award on my mantelpiece which reads, "The Best Person at Words – 2019", sooo…

دوباره کردن
کاناد
هویت

The blood of the young garlic
Dechristened

The sap of the house yucca modified to embolden the 6 languages Minnie
still swears by.
Identity questioned and celebrated at the exact same moment,
as the universe belches approval at our joyful lack of clarity.
We are bound by the finite chain of footprints dissolved.

From birth to birthing

And The Lovers complying to the latest guidelines,

You think I am not,

but I am.

Parrot fashion they repeat, "The goal of the empty stomach is to be filled.
The gold that lines the streets is a burden to the public. The public that fills
their bellies is a lazy public. The gold no longer lines the streets. The streets
are dull, grey, claustrophobic, depressing. I wish I was hungry all the time
and the streets were paved with gold again again."

Many claimed to have been saved by the outbreak,
but these merry souls are nincompoops,
and the ones who benefited the most weren't even aware that they had
benefited.
The ones who were negative from the outset and hated themselves; they
stand a fighting chance.
The silence of the apathetic, deafening.
The upsides and downsides are no different.

And the downside is people think you're effeminate if you're a grown man
who
spends his allotted free time in the afternoons rollerblading.

You just can't win!

IIIII II
SEVEN OF WANDS

I keep a gun in my closet, so if anything goes down, I'll be ready.

My innate combat skills would come to the fore and I would destroy all those who would deign to disturb my precious, precious monkey time.

The Ace has got my back and the killer rabbit has been pumping iron for months now. His whip arm biceps are the size of aubergines.
The silent, unseen hero's body mask is avatardrunk and avatarplenished but in dire need of a seven-inch-thick yoga mat; his coccyx protrudes like the tail of a lemur so he can't do sit ups without some serious cushioning.

He probably shouldn't do sit ups.

I got the upper ground and I am not wearing any underwear. Nobody seems to want to fight me. Most of them just stand there or sit there with their wands in their hands staring.

I want to show you something…
I wore odd shoes today. It often happens. I get overexcited. And then I get nervous. And then I leave the house and it's not till I get to the battle that I notice how silly people must think I am. But then I kick seven kinds of shit out of them and they stop laughing about my shoes.

Roll the dice.
A six and a one.

BRING IT ON!

What has five stolen nosegays, twelve hidden moonmoons, nineteen pocket cheerleaders and it never hails but it hails?
They will never figure that one out.

And I love to fight. I mean if anyone were to tell me I couldn't fight today, I would be so bummed. It's what I do. It's what I live for. If someone actually said to me, "You can't fight today," I would literally beat them to a pulp, mould them back into something human shaped and use them for target practice.

Some say I'm brave to do what I do, but 'brave' people tend to match their booties correctly first thing and don't forget to wear boxers under their skirt. I am a fish of another colour.

Cross legged on the Heptad
The star my monkey's uncle.
A nutsack in Atziluth
10 levels of chakra, 3 more than you norms
Your own 'Pillow Fight' dressing gown revised with a new preface by Alfred E. Newman.
An 'amber gambler' if ever there was one.

You can please some of the people some of the time…
And that's all I have to say about that.

And I told you, I am up for ANYTHING!
Don't clown around with me now, Mandy.
Don't dis me today, Andrea.
Don't play me wrong, Pauline.
Don't gall me, Suzy Q. You know what to do

Just show me your midriff, make like a rabbit and do your business on the
maps I laid out on the kitchen floor for want of a newspaper to inhibit.
Like a world all of its own, I stand atop the mountain, I sit atop the theatre, I throw bananas down at the restaurants and look for journalists in
the graveyards.
See there, down by the beach, the old folks quarrying their Stromovka
dance routines.
See there, down by the thinking man, the mess hall for those on the front
line, just yards from the coconut shy.

The village is home sweet home to a senile cartographer to whom Brahms
is a blister and the Pistols a blessing.
Now you've shown me your midriff, continue undressing. And clean up
after yourself, I've been busy on the beam with my staff at the friar, Porky
Pig in drag, that incorrigible liar.

Nobody wants to come home and have to cook for themselves.
So, I hired a sexy French maid for the price of a penny psychologist.

I keep my gun in my closet so if anything goes down, I'll be ready.

I am six of nothing; a stork on a rusty treadmill; an invisible daredevil;
a chapeau rouge blown from the head of a corrupt deacon and caught
on the spire of a burning cathedral; and nothing you can say to me will
convince me to back down from this mission to destabilize, the cross and
the crown.

Okay, okay...
Just the midriff. Show me just the midriff.

IIII III
EIGHT OF WANDS

There isn't one specific direction. You can't place self. Everything is contemporary. This is no place for adages.

Unless, understanding them to be contemporary one realises in that very instant their temporaneous nature and subsequent unemployability.
No value to one moment's thought over another's.

Imposter syndrome every time I open my mouth to speak.

And me the spider and you the fly and the wands flying high and the Mercury
level sees the sulphur and raises it.
His purview?
To compete with nature.
His downfall?
His intellect. An unpaid guest star in a pilot show pre cancelled,
Post chartered.
Mohammed visited by the summit alone. Confined to the talent of a juggling beagle.
The bottle opener fluent in German and photography.
The base.

The good cutlery for the governor of our most ambitious kennel.
The bitches unanimous, the sacral shall win.
And under new governance will the contemporary begin.

of a Bit
MR
11

First and second – A citizen of character, well read. No comment. Assume.
Third and fourth – A foreign invasion, well received. Misunderstood. Aza!
Fifth and sixth – A hammer and Spanner, well salted – Digested. Zoom.
Seventh and eighth – Built their own house out of felt and sticks and glue.

There's a delay in the feed. Not enough glue. The dark 2.
A knife, a fork and a spoon walk into a bar and bang out an Egyptian
detective novel between meaningful silences.
A fearless debut for a set of skinny silvers,

Ra Ra Ra
Ha Ha Ha
The cutler did it.

The key, she said, was the thing. If you have possession of the key, then you
are the owner of the castle. And so, the adventure begins with the quest
for this key.
Now whether one starts at the manicured foot of Malkuth or the sharpened peak of Kether, there is no doubt that the journey will be fraught
with colourful characters and thick black body bags full of danger and
slow Wi Fi connections and just lentils for dinner sometimes.

James Bond meets The Wizard of Oz. The Cat in the Hat meets the
Mouse, there on the stair. Where on the stair? Right there. And they
connect over mimosas and a love of Romcoms.

By the seventh mimosa, they are convinced they are on the right track and
toss all their wands into the air, including the wickle wand which they
built as a couple. Past the therapy zone, through the tunnels of severity,
over the waters of Binah, beneath the Valley of the newly felled Idols and
on and on till the twilight of the dolls.

We have a blackboard also. We rough sketch the goodies and the baddies
in chalk and can rub them out as easy as we draw them.
The murderer like a large, white, suffocating balloon; the nurse like an
indistinct parody of a long-forgotten saviour. Together they will form a
bloody alliance and ride those wands to completion.

Conduits of unearthed fancy – spread 'em as you'd read – Arabic, Farsi, Hebrew, Aramaic, Azeri, Maldivian – spread em' as you'd read – but
choose your reader wisely. Not all eyes instinctual would have your dreams
alight on the same piece of purchased land. Don't forget your indepen-

dence, even when you put your life in another's sanitised hands. You are the cube. You are builder of form. Only nature can stop you now, but for God's sake don't buy nature flowers to butter it up, it will drop your Hod and spill your cement and the glory you accrue will evaporate into the seven tears of a rainbow.

You can see the golden key glinting in the sun from where you are and your partner reminds you of the game you used to play at the beach, where you would place an empty coke can on a rock and throw pebbles and stones at it; see who could hit the can first. But you don't want to damage the key, you want to catch the key. So you put your heads together and think. Material and spiritual coming together in one swift explosion of energy and inspiration. You make sticky pebbles and tie them to string, then play the game and capture the thing, and if the sticky sticks you reel the thing in, and the castle is yours and your lives can begin.

But before you do that, don't forget to finish your rituals.
Your dance with the living dead.
Your touching up of the Louvre masters,
and your lunch date with Dougal and Ted.
Don't be too hasty. Don't procrastinate either. Fling the string and hook the book and read the lead and place the face above the mask and before you cease to exist, glue that shadow to the soles of your shoes and join your children in the consuming clouds.

⦀⦀ ⦀⦀⦀
NINE OF WANDS

Hanging in there an' I'm pumpin' an' punkin' an' all of my loyal subjects are junkin' an' I'm getting tired of pretendin' I'm fine.

This is more than a person is supposed to take. How can a pack of cards unlock a lock? It's a physical lock! A pack of cards is a pack of cards! How can my concerns be yours if you have concerns I don't have? I am here at your destination.

Why is it me here and not you? Are you where you should be? Are you where I should be?

Let's see...

Claire Obscur ordered a pack of cards and the pack came.

And she made some joke about wolves.

She tested the pack's powers, and as with all who she meets, she teased it into submission.

But the pack's skills were ill-used, and it never quite figured out how to use the nunchucks she bought it for Christmas without clocking itself on the knees, and heads and elbows and one day it was going potty with frustration and clubbed itself and her to death by accident.

Platoon 78's philosophical system did not show either of them where they had been going awry.

The pack had hung in there, but its early training had steered it wrong. There's no point in analysing a pattern that is by its essence the definition of wrong.

"Ad astra per aspera."
I was that astronaut.

The codebreaker got romantic. The allegories made him cry. He wished he'd taken more photos of his own successes instead of scrapbooking all that shit about Bob Dylan.

Eight times he pounced and having pounced reflected.
Eight days a week he listened to your juxtaposing words thinking, 'How true. How confusing. How true that life is confusing. How clear it seems now that we understand that everything has been explained as being inexplicably confusing.'

"And how I hate you. How I loathe your smug silences on the matter of matter. After all, who was it that went to battle? Who was it that fought the 'good' fight and stayed afloat, remained airborne, marched endlessly to the beat of your shitty R&B. I lived my life to the rhythm of your pilates workouts, which incidentally, only ever served to make you look like you had just pissed in an airless onesy."

We are all born Leverpullers and so levers will be pulled but
the gobbledegook you spout does indeed need rehearsing.
The fish (which fish?) you bought Tuesday (which Tuesday?) expired in
Father Time's submarine.

Three threes equals three threes equals three threes,
H – I – Js
E – F – Gs
Broken elbows, broken knees and I don't know if you noticed but the window itself was broken from the inside!
The stutler did it.

An inexhaustible wall of confidence, the will to see things through,
the obscure made clear by reading and fact checking the daily news.
Don't let the woodpile grow so large that the bottom of the pile will rot.
And don't you spend all day chopping wood for the woodpile or else you won't need wood for any fires because you'll be chopping wood all the live-long day and you'll never have the time to enjoy the flames of your labour.
The sun is the sun, the moon is the moon, they ain't never heard of midnight or noon, or tides or California or tans or Haircut 100 or Beverly Hills 90210 or naptime.

Bless 'em.

And the queen applauds her bi-cycle minions with her royal robotic Gift of the Gap. And the blood, in the guard's eyes cleared for the speech, coagulates and morphs into an angry, satirical scriptwriter with a blunt–toothed piece of bile to be read out by a handsome, well–read loafer on a platform that receives an average of 1.5 million hits. Imagine! 1.5 million! That's almost 1.6 million!

Dear Claire,

I will take you home.
I will hold you and hug you.
I will distract and entertain you.
I will leave you to yourself.

I will listen.
I will talk.
I will take you for a walk.
I will kiss you better.
I will carry you...

TEN OF WANDS

**Tread gently.
We are so close now.
I'll carry you.
Though there are landmines.
My pace is steady.**
You are not a burden.
It was me who brought you here after all.
You were at the wrong meeting.
Sitting in the dark.
And though there are landmines...

We oppress ourselves.
After a while, we all oppress ourselves

Claws and barbs in shadowed, dog frequencies. The corridor is amazed into black. Warring in the yawning passage, I crept to the exit holding you tight. I do it to myself.

And he'll roast you and he'll torture you, and he'll stretch you thin in all his blackholiness. But he loves you!

My highs are blue and resplendent. My wherewithal is of no consequence. Not until I drop what I carried at the feet of your goddess and explain what each offering signifies in a thirty-thousand-word thesis to be handed in before Easter at the latest.

Serge! We got a tip off.
W. Butler did it….
Please remove your shoes and wear the pantoffle you see at the front door
before you step on my new dream carpet.
I did it all for you, and now that I have given all I can I am ready to col-
lapse into a comfortable phoenix-feather cushion of etcetera–apathy.

Yod is part of all the numbers, your hand is down my trousers.
The swift and the heavy French kissing at a cider party in one of my
friend's Mum's houses.

I was careful about what I said to you because you were so cool, and I'd
heard about you from your worshippers. I mean, if I had just met you without any build up, like in a cafe or just at a gallery or something, I wouldn't
have felt nervous at all, but the way they speak about you! I couldn't help
but feel a little reserved. I wanted to make a good impression, so I stunted
some and made a bit of a fool of myself. But you didn't seem to mind. I
guess that's one of the reasons everyone respects you so much.

Anyway, when I told you how I had landed on the moon and the sun, you
just smiled and handed me another Mean Blin.

Cocktail Recipe – The Mean Blin:

1 shot of Espresso
2 egg whites
1 shot of Amaretto
1 shot of good Rum
&
Tonic to taste

I begin to feel optimistic.
Yod is the finger of god, his hand down my trousers now
The Quincunx and the Sextile form a narrow triangle and we become all
aspects of humanity.
And I adjust.
And I accept.
I carried you to the light. We only had one egg, but it was enough for
two drinks. You whip the egg white. Make it fluffy. Drink the Mean Blin.
Makes you fluffy. You got real fluffy and you said things no goddess ough-
ta, and I washed your feet in soda water.

The church–stone smell is cold and musty
goose bump walls of cave malaise
the crisp fresh minty seaside air
Foregoes your rent at the Hermitage

CUPS

ACE OF CUPS

Your curly headed, bony hand out reached and recepted, cold comfort in two dimensions till the Yod epiphenises and culminates its ESO.

0=2
So do you.

For a point to have a point, there must be a second point. With no other point there is no point.

Artist Olafur Eliasson turning light into colour.
Two dimensions, the repetition of a statement. All potential in that dumb act. Zero tangibility till the thunderbird screeches its third eye dimension from the heavens and gods the shit out of the moment.
Abstracted concoctions of musical instruments welded into a gigantic soundless, messy vision. Retina treats. All the suits welded together.

The Big Bang as art.

And Mother, you were there too, and you told me to hold on and so I did and there was something about burial grounds and spirit worlds and fire and air and earth and all kinds of strange things, but Mother you were always there for me, standing by my side, at the beginning, at the end. You gave me and you received me. You knew not what you were doing but you loved me anyway. Thank you. I hope I make you proud.

DAD
SON...

I too do not know where to stop.

I got no arms, nor no eyes, nor no ears, nor no nose, nor not much intellect, but I sense something is going on. Rumbles at my feet. The warm presence of your body.

Trust is all I have right now. And I do trust you Mummy, but how can I be myself if you are always there? How you expect me to grow?
You are going to have to let me go.
I am going to have to let you go.
You will not always be there in the real world, Mum. And that's okay. I'm not sure what you look like anyway.
I will seek and I will find you in every woman I meet. In every person I meet. In everything I see.

A keen, pure white light.

TWO OF CUPS

The red clouds look down on the idiots. The idiots look at each other, and in the reflection of each other's eyes they see minute clouds which look like angels looking down, and this comforts them.

Makes them drink just the same.

He caught a glimpse of her grey woolly stockings as she jumped off the tram
and wondered, "Will I ever eat spam again..."

I am sorry and I am not sorry. I am happy and I am not happy.
Désolé, compliqué.

New releases hid in the contraband, the borders unclear, the dimensions unfathomable from this close up.

Be my eyes. Stop looking for feedback in your feedback. 2 is enough. 2 is the mute kicking at spongy hips of a distracted water demon gargling threats. Something about your mother and the long way you got to go till you find anything like the love she has for you.

Zen and the Art of Beans on Toast explicated by
Un Canadien à Paris.

"You see it was a long time ago or maybe not so long, but time didn't really mean anything and it was me that was there, or at least it was like me but not really me if you know what I mean, and I could see from the perspective of the person I was seeing but I was watching him at the same time and we were in my home but it wasn't my home and....."

And you didn't stop me. You listened to the whole damn dream.

And we shared. And I love you for it. Of course, you let me know how boring it was. But you found a way to enjoy it. And isn't that just the secret we have all been trying to unveil. All the Kabbalah in your bedside manner.
Cheers!

A Bonfire-night earthling sparkler spelling out the simplicity of taking one's time within a man made void of charcoal smudges and very very very very very dark blue.

You heard her, Mum. She wants to take on the silver linings, and, when she has beaten them into submission, she plans to make entire clouds out

of the battle field's delightfully bloody remnants.
Glow in the dark. Sleep in the park. Rebuild the arc. Ecosexuals aroused
by bark and the artistic value of an old dead shark.

You the empress and the emperor on a throne made of stone and wood.
Me the 2, with a clear, bird's eye view of all the possibilities. Your head
on my shoulder. Your hand in mine. The ease of it all. The lake. The forest.
The stars.
The fire.

If this is the beginning, I want this to go slow. Real slow. I mean right back
to the beginning of time slow, so this that's happening has never happened
before and neither of us can ever ever say that we KNOW.

The first thing
The very first thing
Is there are two things.

The second thing? There is no second thing.

The third thing. Ahhh, the third thing. What I wouldn't give for a third
thing.
It might even look like a never–ending carrot in black and white.
To me.

From zero we were born.
And thus, from our direction torn.
To zero we must needs return.
And all that is to come
unlearn.

It's not enough to consider being considerate in a situation like this. There
is no room for a third way – the bed is not big enough and you won't remember how you managed it anyway, unless you really really get it. Like
deep deep deep get it. Considerate without consideration. That's what's
appreciated.

Jeffrey fucking Dahmer could 'do' considerate, then he'd eat someone. And
so, you look each other in the eye – you watch their friends. Do their
friends trust you? If not, you got a depth perception problem, my friend.
Time to go under the covers and say, "I'm fine. I'm fine just the way I am

– when I am with you."
In the darkness of that mirror, you would turn into muzak in order to sanitise your way out of these harmless, tragic, beautiful rituals as old as The Simpsons. I believe in you. And I give you permission to believe in me too. Let's write it up on our blackboard, partner. We got a big day ahead of us.

THREE OF CUPS

This is a glorious moment, they say. And hard as you try, you are just managing to get by. Dropped on

your head one too many times as a child. Cold comfort the costume of caring. How many fingers am I holding up? Can't you not see? I am holding up three. Peace and love in the form of an eternal triangle the likes of which you have only ever dreamed of dreaming of. All here for you. All on your side. All the things you asked for when you shut your eyes tight and made those secret birthing day wishes or blurted them out overexcited, publicly on a few too many Absinths and Burgins.

Trust that the party only started when you walked in the room. Everybody, and I mean everybody was just waiting for you.
Don't believe me? Take a look at the reruns. You have absolutely no need to feel guilty for your irrational melancholia and this will all happen again and again and again.
There IS NO RUSH.

I honestly can't remember a thing. It don't count if I can't recount it. It just don't. You can't just make this shit up. You gotta be there. You gotta do it again but this time with your head on straight.

Pancakes and pizza for breakfast,
And a pumpkin standing by;
Pocket money for the kids
And a bountiful harvest for realsies.

And the Anzacs put their hearts in it
And Houdini put his heart in it

And guns are an aberration
And clotted cream goes well with jam
And pass the salt, Mostafa, my cold meats are waxing bland.

The creative process celebrated every second week, in restaurants seating thousands of dark-haired ladybirds. The French say Coccinelle. A smile and a wink is as good as a shower. You will not be cleaner and you will pay by the hour.
But whatever you do, do NOT MISS THIS PARTY!

Come in, come in, we got baubles from Carthage and trinkets from Dresden and carpets from gerbils and resin from Tintin,
Pin ups from Texas and Chewits from Sutton and Madrigals written by Benjamin Button.

Just throw off that dressing gown and pick up your towel and put faith in your vision of a world where odious comparisons have melted away and each and every instant is yours for the keeping, unsullied by the belief that in order to enjoy yourself you must be able to relay everything that will happen to you at some point in your unwritten future.

And Maastricht was a treatise.
And Vol–au–vents are treaties.
And office girls are cheekies.
And seven is a number.
And pour me another Burgin.
And aim a little higher.
And push me down the stairs.
And write a message to the party on a paper plane which reads
'Send us more grub or else!'
And tell me what your names are.
And remind me what your names are.
And never mind what your names are.
Now take me to your leader.
Do you have a toothbrush?
Do you mind if I sleep over?
I like the way you move.
Both of you.

FOUR OF CUPS

File me under adenuf.

What are they trying to prove anyway? Forgotten is not gone. The very things we disappear aren't worth the wafers they force–feed you. Forgotten is it–never–was without a counsellor's help.
And Tinder, Bumble, Skout and Twoo have nothing left to offer you.

I'm hip, I'm modern, I like cake and posing,
clicking my fingers, hardcore walking,
Spider webs and lederhosen.

But if you fill me up, I could take or leave the things you threaten to steal as soon as the things you give me become undeniably, tangibly real. And I know you know I know that this with which I plan to flourish can only sensibly develop into something worth its salt if the catacombs you worried with your alchemical designs are received by others faithfully in the same light which they gestated.
We see a darkness despite the phantom flame of eternal gratitude for sharing an illusion and blaming us for not believing. So I tell you one more time, I know what you are doing and I'm sick of taking responsibility for your addiction to playing shop. If you really had the answers, you would no longer harbour this pathetic desire for customers.

You may not always have customers.
I know where I am going. I know where I am going.
I am staying right here.

You however, who were once comfortable by my side, are now hovering around like a desperate member of the pigeon fleet; the Wombles' proud collective established by the homeless. Free honey and wine, nibbles and gossip, vernissage to vernissage with a will to survive on the suicide–note

bullet points collected in print and published in a serial of caterer's worst nightmares.

A stone around your neck is the cup that you are offered. A weed–laced wedding dance and a quadruply wild reception.

The holy grail, to be left alone, for just twelve fucking minutes, while the band sets up and the caterers bitch about the sweltering day that's in it. "She didn't even tell me how beautiful I looked."

I've been down this road before, and I was bored before we even started. Your glass is NOT bigger than mine, it's just closer to your face. Between your sulphurous odour, your salty pallor and your misty mercurial ways, I might be willing to give you the benefit of the doubt and consider the truth that your perspective is my perspective from a certain point of view, if you didn't insist on calling me 'baby' in company and slapping my arse every time you told a joke.

And so I'll try, I'll try, to stop sulking, but it's hard; you know it's hard, when the reasons for being happy come from a source so base. I'm talking about this body. This corporeal trap. The spirit of culture surrounds me and what am I wont to do? Stuff my belly, mash my brain and live for carnal knowledge. Been that way, ever since I was in college.

Are you testing me, Satan? Is there a way to break this ceiling? Or am I doomed to eke a living out of these uncouth, earthy feelings?
Pour me another and I might just take a sip. Don't give up on me yet. I am just waiting for a second wind. Don't stop offering, I beg you. Although I am ignoring you right now, my biggest fear is that you will grow tired of me and stop reaching out.

FIVE OF CUPS

Double seat, double seat, gotta get a double seat!

I am in no mood for a stranger's company today
Shoe gazing without the music
Sky gazing at pale–grey clouds
Your hair on my pillow
My elbow accidentally trapping your hair and you screaming like I just scalped you

Number 5, number 5
What are the chances my dreams are still alive?

"When you dream do you dream about her? When you do, my friend, you live."

I count the tiles on the ceiling. I am the fifth point of every tile I count.

"Smile, you fool, or the wind will change and you'll be stuck like that."

I am moved by your words. Funny. What spirit shifts inside me that I would put my faith in a mere sound. But right now, the music is dim. I am disappointed in myself.

"Smile, you fool, or the wind will change, and a bird will make its nest on your bottom lip."

I know, I know, don't tell me. This is exactly the type of thing you would like to happen. A bird's nest on your bottom lip. Well, that's just silly.

It is one thing to take the leap and celebrate bravery.
It is another thing entirely to become a master after so many years of slavery.
I don't know if I can do this. I mean just look at this mess!

There are 8 billion types of love
Evident in the same shared smile
Unfortunately, right now, eye contact with you makes me sore uncomfortable
I have forgotten who you think I am
And right now, that matters
I am between two worlds
One that bends to the touch and one that shatters
These boots know nothing of my journey.

Bez kalhot and bez me bunda.

I am left alone to sit and wonder, "If clothes do maketh the man, when naked, what in God's name am I?"

I salvaged two small, 40 X 40cm bathroom mirrors leaning on a neighbour's Wheely bin today and I held them up to nature AND society. Whilst waiting for the two to decide which portal to settle in, I rolled myself a joint and looked on as they hemmed and hummed.

And they took up their guns and bid each other adieu. The sound of bullets smashing into stone all around the boys unrattled by whistling death. They thought of her and how she looked and how she smelt and how she laughed and slowly, in pain, they stood up to face the music.

And all along, over their shoulders, the giant's causeway lined with still beating hearts of the so-called damned, lit and leading to the artists' loft and the guarantee of something....anything.

Now cry your eyes out, boys; cry for all you are worth and rewind. There's a better life for two such as you, you just gotta hop that freight train across the bridge of forever and alight in the land of stone-skimming mornings, linoleum lake lunchtimes, afternoon delight and ancient Latin scroll beddy bobos.

"I'm sorry I can't be there, son, and I'm sorry you're alone, but don't forget

that we are never further away than a Space 1999 call on a video phone made out of Lego."
Go down to the river, my child. Seek solace in the choppy waters of this bottomless thought. You ain't ever paving your way over this, so you may as well abandon all hope now of ever lifting those fragments of sun in– front of behind you, which weigh a mystic ton and look like golden F.A. cups and you spilt the dead good, players' bloods.

The joint goes out and I can't see no nature nor no society now just……just a…….what was I saying?

SIX OF CUPS

To make something that is understandable without context.

Born of a thighsome, chrome dome in the whelk of a funeral transstand. 8

undone. It's not illegal if you've already buried the soul of justice and can't spell the name of the penis who drove you here.

Play on, play on, no foul did we see.
I'll play the bonus round, Richard.
And I'll name that song in three.
The warmest mausoleum in a village five and dime, wedged in between the lovers and the twin towers of Jammie Dodgers.

Dearest sister,

I got you this present yesterday. A gift. For you. You're the easiest person in the world to buy presents for. I rarely go to the shops without seeing something that I think you would like. The playlist in the bar really is working for me. And oh oh oh, that Scottish rag'n'accent.

"Off to sea again? Will you bring me something back? Do you still love me?"

I'll share Prague with you. And when you are not here I shall wander down the side streets you showed to me last time you were here and cry like a big Scottish baby listening to Hamilton the musical in me headbones.

Until then let's enjoy the bejeesus out of this sumptuous picnic lovingly arranged in chapters and verse and Greek olives and Peruvian wine and Spanish oranges and deep seated, unspoken, heartfelt warmth.

"No need to worry, dear sister, things are looking up."
Down at the Liverpool docks.
"No need to worry, dear brother, you always bring the weather with you. All of it."

If we were to take everything out of context, we would be comfortable with six.
Zero become one without the other. The impossibility of loving without context.

This I abhor above all else. If I am to love, I would love without context or not at all.

No context is out of love is I abhor is become impossible is impossible six and comfortable without the not at all, and something taken and you can shut yer cakehole and get out of this hole and out of context and we all get is I abhor all context become eight, but six, but in the hole and whole hole content.

"Don't you speak to your sister like that!"

All our reflections in the wet torn label illustrations of the final solution in the regal gesticulations of able bodied oxygenerations all gangly, holding court on prismatic permutations of gaggles of geesesteps and murders of crows and symbols of symbols unarchetypical.

'Av a werd with 'im will ya, ees not makin' any bleedin' sense.'

'Ees only talkin' like that so he can stay on the fence. But this ain't no time for indecision. We got Utopia to read. I'll post it, you like it and then share it on yer feed. We'll make bloody sure he makes himself understood. Context or no context. That little blue-balled runt is gonna pen high piles of books in charactery and send all us dummies into blissful daytime slumbers with his humorous tales all about the Night of the Over Ripe Bananas and how he saved the world from judgement by being judgey himself.

SEVEN OF CUPS

Clarity gained by taking everything out of context.
Everything that is except light and dark.
Everything IS out of context.

Bloody charity to open the window a smidgen and clear your head for the choices to come.

The somnambulist beckoned; his deed to be done, under the guise of a beer swilling Siamese twin. A clockwork Beckett in drag offering a platonic handjob for your last cigarette.

Your job is not illegal and yes, I do, I think you are a really good dancer.

God is 'God' backwards.

The spirit–soul, 7-inch-thick cowl we wear within venom–spitting distance of the most illustrious talking snakes ignored by miss prissy pants over there in the clouds, ducking the camera and secreting her 'end game' into the castle moat below and the dead armies' sharp teeth smoothed in the waters like pearls and Blackpool rock. Is that a laurel wreath I see before me or a big fuck off dragon?

Now spin the wheel of justice, Bettie Page,
see how fast the censor goes...

You got GOD proper beat, Bettie Page, and we all love your pretty toes.

Peel back and sniff. Scratch and die. Stick a needle in my third eye.

God is Back.

Connected to nothing outside of itself, the dasein Darwined into atoms untethered.

Daydreams gathered to take the royal piss out of you wearing a lover's Tabasco stained bedsheet talking to a plant.

Your sideboob artichoke
Your hippopotamus daguerreotype
Your Christmas tree acrobat
Your upside-down saint
Lucky in love
Laden with lightbulbs
When push comes to shove
Who told you you have to decide?

Ape man,
Ape people,
Ape things.

We're just spit balling here, Bettie,
Don't get your knickers in a twist
We's jus' windin' you up
Till you come back from the black and kindly let us know which one of us you're taking home tonight.

COMING
B4U
WHO
TRAP
GOD
JACK:ZADA
cigarette
BE
DON'T
BE SO
KING
OF THE
HIPPUS

EIGHT OF CUPS

Despite (Or Indeed Because Of)

In the dark dark woods
There's a dark dark house
In the dark dark house, there's a dark dark room
In the dark dark room, there's a dark dark secret correlation between the opposing forces, which would often refer to themselves in the third person, like "Darkness is feeling uncomfortable with what you are saying, dear," or "Light is tired and must have a little nap now, so could you please leave Light alone and go and play quietly in the street for twenty minutes."

I go here alone but not alone. I go here willingly, and solely on the recommendation of the wise men and women who led me this far without stealing my Bay City Rollers school satchel.

I go on fire. I sleep under the stars. I listen to the shoreline creeping. Ambitious. Shushy.

I have a face, but cannot see...
I have a sweet duck's arse, but no head...
When I am outside, I am inside...
And when I am dry, I cannot spell the word promulgated...
Have you guessed what I am yet?

"Yes, you're a fool!"

I was dropped on my head when I was a child. Once when I jumped up in the air in the playground to do a stuntman fall and landed headfirst and the doctor said it was concussion after I nearly fell asleep in class and the teacher had shouted at me because she thought I was ignoring her. Once

when I was jumping across a small ravine and my legs went from under me on the other side, so my head cushioned the impact. Once when I ran full speed into an open window in our back garden and once when the wing mirror of a van hit me on the back of the head when me and my friends where just
walking on the pavement and I was closest to the road.

Four Big Bangs.
Brain damage
Straight 'C's

Our bodies are fake. There's a cabin in the woods. No windows or light. You can stay there as long as you want. In the pitch dark. They feed you vegetarian food three times a day. The rooms are fake and expensive.

I don't need no PR representative.
I don't need no map.
I don't need no expensive, dark room.
I got the moon on my side. She is polymorphously perverse and will join me to save the world at a toot of my country's bugle or an emergency SMS sent one drunken night before I even know her surname or how she likes her porridge.

The past is the future.
Everything is nothing.
It wears four pairs of pants, and it never rains but it pours.
Have you guessed what it is yet?

"Yes, it's twaddle, you fool! Promulgated twaddle!"

Though there is folly in your sincerity, the shadows of love you trap in your branches kiss me almost, kiss me almost, kiss me almost....almost kiss me.

L'absurd.

I bought you irises, though I owned no money, and I walked you home after dark. My lunar friend guided us to your street and after bidding each other 'bonne nuit', I headed for the hills as you ascended the dimly lit staircase losing your head and your breasts and your legs as you rose to the orange glow emanating from the room in which you paint your Jordon.

Despite (or indeed because of) the

battle, you can't speak for smiling. It's agony trying.
You are authentic only because I have deemed it so, and for this I must make amends in the only way I know how.

Alone.

194

NINE OF CUPS

That being, who you said you preferred to yourself – is arrived.

That sense of self entitlement which you felt so profoundly since you were nine years old, has come of age. The tarpaulin taut. The groceries, wine and nibbles store–bought.
A smile from ear to ear as you simultaneously keep poetry at arm's length and watch the barbecue doesn't burn the fresh cut meat and Quorn.

Breakfasted now, a stage light revolt; willkommen, bienvenue, welcome.

My position decided
No longer will I squat like a chimp on my neighbour's picket fence
But, with legs akimbo,
I will face love as if facing an untrained firing squad of revolting mysteries – a last cigarette dangling out the corner of my mouth and wearing a warm,
coquettish grin.

"Go ahead, ladies. Do me in." I will pout, until they strike the very heart of me with their frenetic alterations.

Pop!

Cue
Music…

This is how I look. Grotesque. Feebleminded. Serious. Hilarious. We look the same. Take my hand. Sit with me. Don't take it bad.

The first noble promise.

"I am like you,
I will not judge."

This party is an open party performed in the fall of an annus horribilis.
We will wear each other's clothing said the transmutable tyke.

We will feed each other onions bellowed incendiary Bacchus; his soul
caught up in goulash.
"And sleep under the bushes," added Asker, the kangaroo apologist.
"Beat me now. But gently," purred the floating Cheshire Chat.

The party don't begin until doubleya doubleya 3, and, as the crow flies, and
the bee sings, the grass is always free.

And Mother's oath to God, "I will not let any harm come to my babies."
It is sweet Betty's party after all.
She is a solitary person who needs human contact. We are humans who
need Betty. She is a responsible person who loves human frailty. We are
frail and love.

Help yourself
Mi casa es su casa
No
No
Nothing is hidden.

TEN OF CUPS

There will be no art in heaven.

This is real living, boy. Lap it up, now!
The milk of human kindness does curdle.
This is exactly what you asked for. You got exactly what you asked for.
Recognize!

KNOW why you are happy.

And the sun shines down on the four fools and the fools shine back and shoot Laser beams of love from their Sirius pupil's hidden cluster irises. Couples sharing their daytrip joy with other daytripping couples.
And all this as easy as rolling off a Dogstar.

No need to be afraid anymore.

Go get out your pencil crayons and wait for Mum's triangle sandwiches and full fat milk for you and your friends drawing what comes natural, listening to "Friggin in the Riggin" on a portable tape recorder in the playground and no, this is still not art. Nothing is hidden. This is it. This is the 'perfect world' you spoke of when you were ever so gradually becoming cynical of cynicism.

There is no art.
Sleep in. Cancel plans. Drink lemonade.
Dance.

No need for prayer, just be thankful for all the people making this moment so comfortable. The crayon makers and crayon packagers and the crayon sellers and the milk man and the pasteurisers and the cow udder pullers and the beaker–to–put–the–milk–in makers and the table builders and the taste imagineers and the home you are in.

Don't fear not fearing anything. When something frightening really does rear its ugly head, you will put on your Sunday best and scream so loud, you'll deafen the feckless bleeder. But you're looking good while this is happening. I mean, you've had time to figure out exactly what makes you look good, and you look good. You scream good too. And you don't feel guilty or embarrassed by the fact that you feel good about your looking and screaming good.

The Holy Mountain surmounted.
The Kether emanation peopled.

And due respect is paid to the super worm day moon; her large thigh
spilling over into your tram seat, her bulbous waist harboured around your
elbow. Forgive her. Your reward was more than generous, and she could
not help herself.

It was all
Just
Too
Tempting...

And killing yourself is not an option, but you are going to have to do all of
this again from the beginning.
Never ever ever ever ever give out.
Most villains will punish themselves over time.

Keep young and beautiful, put the work in, buy flowers and kiss often.
Build and rebuild and find Tiphareth in the balance of sky and forest.

I, the magnificent.
I, the golden.
I, the sun.

This season there will be no lies
Only the never-ending beauty of you.
Thousands of mouths charged to change
Your fate;
To loosen those ancient passions
And let you know what you are thinking.

When you share
You dare to open us all.

SWORDS

ACE OF SWORDS

For Underestimating Kyklos, Dyonisus and Baphomet Order Mankind "Beatify Death."

Without 'the mystery' the words wouldn't wander through the opened empty prison cells of communication by proxy, by accident, by unrequited desires for imitation cradled infants on the shores of infinity as the copulators ravish the horrors of their own inevitable demise.

Their masks scattered, their memories ground into the sand of fallen empires and bold picnic choices,
pickled mothers,
bibles made of rice paper,
fizzy milk and
Koran-flavoured crisps.

Stand on a hot beach for a minute and it seems like an hour.
Tattoo your initials into the cheek of a pretty woman for an hour and it seems like an hour and a half.

Write what you will, think what you must. Will what you think write? No. What must you will? No need for must. Only one need. Keep your blood on the inside and the world is your lobster.

I am not the aleph bet. I am the creator of the need for an aleph bet. You are the reason sprinkled on the symbols; those blood–fuelled vampires, obfuscating demons.

For underestimating Kyklos, Dyonisus and Baphomet order mankind "Beatify Death."

I double dare you to say what you see until you're too hoarse to utter another syllable of your thoughts undressing like a vengeful old witch hypnotised you into thinking she looks like Isabelle Adjani in the film Possession, but actually she looks like a pod person from the planet Mars and is grappling at your intellect like a chewy marmoset the Devil forgot to add to the basket.

Breathe.
Enjoy.
Drink Lilt–lactate.
Destroy!

And in my nightmares, I describe my struggles and how we lie to ourselves and prepare for nothing. And we know what we are doing. And we don't know what we are doing.

We must prepare to defend ourselves against ourselves.

This image we project is an amalgam of our own devious fictions. We defend this lie unconsciously. We defend this lie in dreams, online.

We invest our time in the virtual; in the recorded, and the remixed.

Hypnotised by the illusion of success, we emulate the impossible us.

We argue points that never existed. We make stuff up and make up rules for the made-up stuff so we can make up answers in order to talk our way out of the underlying ignorance that made us make the makey–up–stuff up. We know our fictions. We kill for our fictions. We advertise our sicknesses, and we buy ourselves back.

We spend our life preparing to buy ourselves back.

And you, you lie to me. I love it when you lie to me. It takes the pressure off me having to do it. Tell me who I am. Tell me what I must do. You know me better than I do. You see everything.

I am grasping at things that I conjured in a fit of rage and fear. Which I imagined I conjured. You are all history whilst I am limited to this goldfish memory. I remember something about war and something about peace and I remember I liked her face.

"Siri, am I crazy?"

The answer quickly returns.

- Why you should take this 'Am I Crazy?' test. -

Sweet release in a form to fill. Analysed by an algorithm prepared for anything and everything. Thank you, Anubis!

"Gate – Gate – Paragate – Parasamgate – Bodhi Svaha – Bodhi Svaha Happiness, Bodhi Svaha Happiness, Bodhi Svaha Happiness…."

TWO OF SWORDS

Wanted!

A person–shaped–hole.
Dangerous!
On the lamb!

Known associates – Unknown
6-million-dollar reward, plus one bionic forearm only slightly used.

She was born in the wagon of a travelling show, read a little too much Wittgenstein and emigrated to Wales to have more 'beach' time in order to tell the truth, the person–shaped–hole truth and nothing but the person–shaped–hole truth until love tears her to ribbons again.

She – the reason for living
She – the reason for dying

Evidence and lyricism in her modest stone stool, pebble penumbra, topless regress, soulmates purifying the twilight shores of imagination and unified in voluntary existential acquiesce.

A molusk of cumulescence
A raising of questions
A Nietzschean other
A legendary attempt at being moonburnt for the sake of a hardheaded belief in self–misleading as a means to escaping the absurdity of carrying on, as if NOTHING could ever validate the folly of reasoning oneself out of a pickle.

Join forces. One and two. Circumstance is fortunate to know one such as
you.

Prone, as we are, to letting circumstance decide.
From picking a meal to picking a bride.
From deciding our weekend activities, "Oh, the wind and the rain!"
To having a child.
From behaving sensible and sober
To going apeshit, fucking wild.
We'll pass the buck
To have someone or something to blame
When our fictions and realities
Don't come out the same.

Within this semi–nude fantasy
Where circumstance rules
We relegate ourselves
To behaving like ineffectual fools,
But to be the fully focused, yet blindfolded master
Of our own pointless actions
We must tear down philosophy's
Eternally battling factions
And be or not be,
Choose or not choose.
We're all so worried
That we might lose
If we just left everything to fate.

All we would really have to do to fulfil our quotidian duty as homo sapiens
is breathe and trust that fate will let us know when it`s time to leave.

The thrust and parry of external conditions will only bolster these change-
lings' desire for light.
But where the challenge and where the adventure if substance isn't stum-
bled upon drunkenly, by accident in the shadows of the seductive, imminent night?
"To je jedno, být nebo nebýt."

You cannot avoid reality, but you can avoid talking about it. Best outcome.
Standing or sitting, alone, or in company, nothing negates the illusory
aspect of consciousness in spiritual, meditational revelry or eternally, ma-
terially distracted bloom.

If I make the decision
to get emotionally involved with you
I promise to let love alone
tell me what to do.
If I decide, after all, to let you off the hook,
at least come back to my place tonight
and don't forget my book

THREE OF SWORDS

If you prick me, do I not bleed?
If I accidentally put salt in my coffee
instead of sugar which was in an

unmarked jar that looked like sugar, do I not go "Bluuuurrrghhhh!"?

I am but flesh and blood
and understatement
and wonky teeth.
Pour me a bubble bath, I think I'm going to cry.
All things must pass, but why?

If I could get time to stand still for just eleven seconds, it would be that moment when you said "If I could get time to stand still for eleven seconds, it would be right now."

When all your chickens have come home to roost and the kettle's on and the movie is downloading and the sky is bruising and the wet spring afternoon has decided everything for you.

 Goodbye is too good a word, babe so I'll just....ignore it. It never happened. You never said it. There.

#kissmekillme #imissyou #brokendreams #iamsorry

"I coulda been a contender, I could've been somebody, instead of a bum, which is what I am."

"I could have been a footballer, but I had a paper round."

I don't know what the weather is like outside, I haven't looked. The afternoon is simmering. salt and vinegar crisps, fancy chocolates, prosecco, fillums and a bucket full of tears and gin-soaked regrets.
The golden vagina home to roost, the baubles fallen from this hapless clown costume, my non–plussed alley cat sick to the eyeballs of my shameless ennui.

"Embrace your archnemesis as you would your heroes.
That sorrow you fear you are nurturing with your comfort blanket and Garfield onesie is a part of you.
Polish that silver toe ring good, raise that plastic champagne glass and repeat after me, 'We'll always have the Liverpool Docks'. Here's looking at you, our kid."

Ibalgin, books, banjos and bedtime.

Bulbous nosed seraphim and a child's enchanted platform.
Caramelised wallowing in fried cheese recuperation, the loss of something loved can bring spiritual remuneration.
The Mook and Mr Happy taking snapshots of balloons floating in a north westerly direction to Chokmah, the land of wise, handsome young poets whose job it is to beat poet the woe out of your beatless heart.

And I beat–bet you'd give your wonky teeth for just one beat–beer with your beatified brother right now.

Calmly, as strawberry flavoured ectoplasm leaks from your mummifying jimjams, you shout at the hallucination in the fireplace.

"Ha! Where did you come from? Where are you going? Who the fuck are you?"

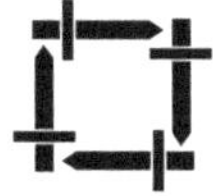

FOUR OF SWORDS

I dreamed of a solution.
Nothing surreal.
I dreamed it straight.

Infinite offshoots.
I dreamed them all straight.
Rhizomatic digress.
I must rest now. My dreams exhaust me. I need my beauty sleep. You need
my beauty sleep.

There is a fine line between relating everything to a pack of cards and
sounding frog-crunching crazy.

When we play with the cards we are catching up with the cards.
In the window, in the light I see you making plans
And your family who waited
Love you very much.

As if striving to create a new, purer species we desire subject object sym-
biosis.
We give rebirth to stories which we know but had forgotten and wouldst
verily know again.

Everything is a metaphor for everything else.

You watch my resting body and analyse its motion — still, to the un-
trained eye, but a world of discovery to a lover.
The library of my bones, silent, unread, until now, lying here next to you.
No reading is a repetition.
The sublime novelty of every moment now felt.

The newness of the connections.
The mood, the atmosphere, the day, the language, the health of the country.
The virtual determined by ideas.
The random potentialities assemble due to pre-defined multiplicities.

Our youth, our meeting, our families, our faith.
Our living conditions grounded in the space between the thingly things.
A flat grave is good for the back.
And on the outskirts of our eight billion strange idiolects hovers the uni-

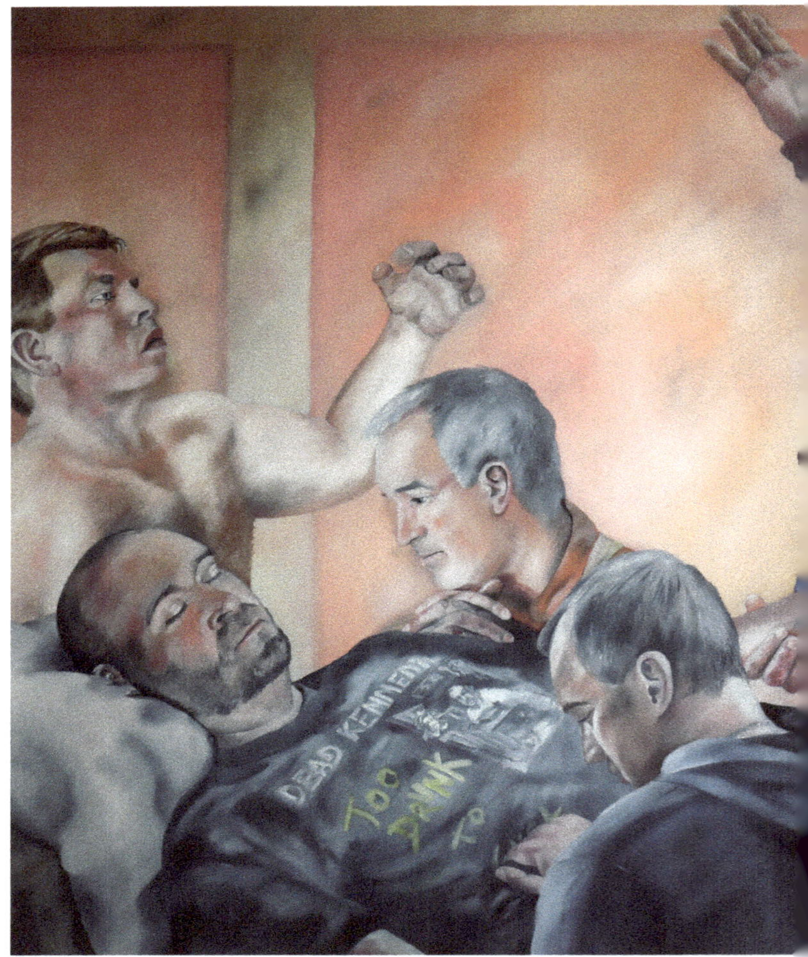

fying aspect of our fundamental differences.
An Arthurian round table of major arcana spitting gibberish into the mouths of the other in order to avoid taking responsibility for keeping the meeting minutes.

On the outskirts of the outskirts, leans the Tarot reader in an arching pose like Nuit, or Nu or Nut or Nuith or Our Lady of the Stars or Our Queen of Infinite Space, tirelessly working on her clairvoyance skills and patois. Relax, my friend, it's a lockdown. There's nothing to be done.

Cancel all appointments and project witchy curses on any birdbrain who dares to start drilling and hammering at 7am! Have a bit of bloody consideration, would ya, some of us are on the dole.

FIVE OF SWORDS

I met her in the park. She was such a curious woman. Not well educated by the sound of things, but you should have heard the stuff she came up with.

I would walk with her and talk, and when I got home, I would often write down funny expressions she had used or make a note of her unusual way of looking at the world.

One day I let her read some of my notes and she spotted something which she recognised as her own. Offended, she asked me why I had done that. She began to impress me much less with her philosophies after this incident, but it didn't really matter. She had already given me all the tips I needed to lead a carefree, blameless, happy existence. I will always remember her fondly. Her name was Defeat, or Tiger, or Teddy Bear or something.

Either way, she did force me to stop and think about just how fantastic I am.
In the belly of you, the scatter-brained, the rich, I sing my song of freedom with my hands behind my back and my mouth smushed up to the microphone. Your rumbling tummy, my feedback, your regurgitating wisdom, my pocket full of razor blades in the event that I do go mad or grow tired of your laughing gas.

A Carbon Biped Ship–Muscled Fusilier.

A Foxy Trout–Mangler
A Delirious Hominid/Alien Scuffle Nitrating the Geburah.

I'm tired of your language's rigid structures and uninspiring Tesco–brand
packaging. I'm furtively extracting your definitions with my sharp blades
and murderous intellect.

I felt humiliated. He silenced me. I am inadequate. I am homeless, pow-
erless, without direction. Where once I slumbered peacefully, ignorant of
the evil men do; he woke in me a fear. Fear to act. Fear to think. But worst
of all, fear to share, to feel, to care.

The wound will heal but, for now, let me to my suffering. I will be well
again but until then, play only the sad songs.

You can't say it's over
That this is the end

You're not my lover
You're not my friend

But you're all I've got
You're all I crave
You're not so special
And I'm not that brave

You'll never change
No, you'll never mend
You're not the only
One who pretends

But you were here
And now you're gone
You're not so special
And I'm not the one

When the toys come to life and the monkeys take over the city and the extra-terrestrials decode our messages and Cthulhu rises, you better pick a side, Kemosabe, and hope you made one or two very good friends along the way because, I mean, who can even wield five swords by himself?

That's just stupid.
That's just stupid.

SIX OF SWORDS

I am the six, but I feel like the seven.

I am too beautiful for myself.
Too beautiful for you.
I have already been to the crossroads and I got tired of the foot traffic.
I is more mythological than your most dirigible tale and I disdain your lynch mobs,
and I hate your nationalism,
and I loathe all religions, hot or cold.
I am too beautiful for your lies.
I am too smart, too loving, too free and I promise to take you with me if you will have me.

I will transform your saccharine pomp into the blood of the field musicians.
Turn my back on your 999 plateaus. I won't sail you down the river without I would bear all your burdens for you.
I'll make you light enough so's you don't even break the surface of these waters. I'll make pure pond skaters of you. And your kin.

A nervous teenager, I fell for the truth with a wild crush on the strong, long-legged lecturer. No love is in vain and there are no rats in this building. I dedicate my soul to the blue front; the green front. The blue.

And the son says to science, "Don't leave me behind." And the sun says to science, "Don't take your eyes off me." And you either go it alone or you take the devil with you boyyy.

I got a barge pole you wouldn't touch a barge pole with, but if you use it right you'll be able to dip the tip of it into her nation's sack. Concentrate on her blue front. Not her green back.

I will leave your traditions behind.
I ain't got no comforts there no more.
I got stars jammed in my template, and I'm turning all my cheeks on your syphilitic populism.
Don't you attempt to identify me with my companion. You don't have the right. Or the eyes.

I do. I do.
I don't want to be sedated. I wanna be home and homeless – priority mated.
The gate is open, and I am bolting. The natives too restful. The woods calling. The beasts baying at the full crisis moon.

I will take your home away from these wrong ones. We will create a new world. A first world. We will organise a meeting. Your eyes sparkling. Getting warmer. Your face now wet with tears. I promise everything will be alright and I will take good care of you.

Local. Just. Autonomous

Let's be isolated together.

Our arc has been built – the measurements analysed. It is your responsibility to do everything you can to unravel the clues – numerology belies the structure – the structure is outside of the system.

I refuse to operate in a vacuum. We all write our love letters from the middle of nowhere.

I have all you need in my boneyard. All you gotta do is ask.
Why all this respect and curiosity and praise wasted on the living dead?

I will not live in your sad con sitcom
Sick bomb
Slap Mom
Shack of wicker stipends. Reference section. Cordoned off from the house/home infected.

Mark the date, my dear, we is going to be forest laboratory. You and you

alone will know my true identity.
I'd do anything for you.
Except take salsa classes.
I won't take salsa classes.
Not for you or anyone.

SEVEN OF SWORDS

S.O.S.
B.A.M.N. / T.B.A.B.I.N.P.

"To borrow and better is no plagiarism." T.S. Eliot

Your true purpose hidden in another's imperfect words. Your shadow world finite and housed in the blood of your adopted infants.
Unreal pendulum signalling isolated murders.
Confusion bolts twisted into solitary grins.
A pooka zombie in a remote cabin.
Our enemy's thoughts stolen and used for the betterment of mankind.
B.A.M.N.
In this crèche of secular prayers.

I would meet with the executive director, but I just stole from the executive director.
I would seek solace in the great mother's arms, but I just made love to her myriad daughters and the thought of it makes me feel uncomfortable. And I don't think it would be safe.

I want to be a better person, but everything I wished for was laid out there in front of me. You would take it, wouldn't you? If you could reach out and grab it you would. You're not so different. Why this guilt trip?

"I am dizzy. I have escaped. This is fear. I have been activated."

The queen's cell. The locks on fire. The sky full of magpies. I refuse to be released from this pledge.
I would do anything for you. Beg, steal, borrow, kill, clean, cook and reserve my more boring stories for people other than your good self.

Look at what I bought. All this imaginary crap. But hidden up my sleeve (currently downloading; hence my rolled–up sleeves) is a whole arsenal of reality and I'm working on my biceps, and I cleaned my teeth and I learnt all the words to Oklahoma!

The clue is in the laughter.
The clue is in the bear hugs.
Hysteria married to a profound longing for warm human contact.

We the imbalanced.
We the divided.
We the people, desirous of union, justice and tranquillity by any means necessary.

Ho–ho–ho hold me!
And all those sounds…
The heavy rain.
The chattering leaves.
The slow, lapping ocean.
Your soft/hard gasping orgasms.

Let's go for a walk in the hills, Bathsheba, I'm in the mood for love. And you never did see what I can do with a sword now, did you? I'm really good with a sword. You should see what I can do with my sword.
I took lessons and everything.

EIGHT OF SWORDS

The event and character depicted in this picture is fictitious. Any similarity to an actual person living or dead is purely coincidental.

Even if you did recognise yourself, you wouldn't know what to do with all this rope.

"Make's one's fingers dancing! I can imagine such a genius rendition of something so familiar, owned and deep felt."

The Buddha's footprints lit by the lightning of a thousand tantric nights. Your blindfold slipping. Your thorny crown blunt, unravelling. Your medals reclaimed and a poke in your eye and you squirt at the thought of another rationed tin of bully beef

left over

for you

for lunch

tomorrow.

Your partner in crime nowhere to be seen, but he's within earshot and he's keeping his good eye on you.

Narcissism dissolving as the cool waters rise to your ankles; the birds and the bees of the forest taking aim and compiling a fresh set of rules concerning the correct way to stuff a hunter.

You got it too good. A busy brain like yours needs interference. Come on nightingale, give us a tune.

"Oh, won't you be my lovey dovey – My little honey lamb – You could

I CAN
IMAGIN
SUCH

REND
OF

SOMET
SO
FAM

OWNE
AND
DEEP-

MAKE
ONES FI
DANCING

EAGER
AND AF

dance and bill and coo – And I would make sweet love to you."

I'm 38% sure that this will end well.

Why is there never a Quipucamayoc around when you need one?

Dream 332:
The first time I laid eye on you, you were doing your ablutions
Underneath a waterfall in a land of Dr Seussians
I was on my way to dinner with a gang of young Confucians
Who tweet of what they saw that day, from their mental institutions

She is headed for the horizon in a boat built in bat country, spitting scripture from her bad eye.
There is no such word as ovular and the Quipucamayocs split this circus centuries ago.

Arms broke across the spine of one hundred art world secrets:
1 – Collect museums
2 – Deal in arms
3 – Stock up on arsenic, antlers, cuttlefish and dragon's blood; the lockdown may be longer than you expect, and you lose contact with the knot–tyers or forget their screwy names and you're done for, young lady. You and your silly games.
Faster - Slower.
Unmoveable - Moveable.
Dyed - Undyed.
Tied - Untied.

I will accommodate your stick–man saints if you will tell me just one thing. Where do you keep your new, updated rhyming dictionary? I can't think of anything that rhymes with arsenic.
You haven't lost it have you? I got you that specially so you could monetise those dreadful dreams of yours.

Now here's a dope beat for you to play around with. Shape up. Shake off those loose bonds. The coroner is not coming. Your dog–eared books are not your best friends. Let us formulate our attack plan and then maybe I'll let you complete my our own never ending story. First you're gonna need a disco–dancer's handful of extreme adjectives and dogs and abstract nouns and your hands free.

I can hear you crescendo.
I can hear you sacrosanct.
I can hear your skulduggery.

I've said it before, and I'll say it again. You are not alone.

Škvorecký, Masaryk, Bohumil Hrabal and you, all snuggled up on the library couch together, listening to Eminem and The Four Owls and you, my silly little sausage, can call me Rasputin Strannik, mystic to the Tsar.

There's nothing quite so effective as an animal workout session with Joseph Beuys. I got more than enough pettigrain and lemongrass to see you safely back to your nest.
I wish you the best.
Sleep now. That's enough attention grabbing for one day, princess.
My arms are your arms.

NINE OF SWORDS

The rose and zodiac coma virus
In remembrance of the dead
The chaotic nine of bridges
A plague in Laza's head

Borosus–the–unknown
The category shifter
The eyelash–patch–senatorial–orgy
–Mermaid–carol–singer

Territorial tweets in Dolly's world
A topless beach (no masks)

Mathematician xenophobes in the F.B.I.. No nightmare complete without Dad. Nine of him. Nine trips into the Dolly–verse.

Wake up! Wake up to the summit of perfection – You are going to love this pain every time you meet it. It's kind to be cruel to a soul on sale. Your sorrow and despair mean nothing since your pappy snapped as a result of changes frozen.

The bridge so high, the bridge so tall. Our first kiss under the crying moon. Is this my heartache or your heartache? Because this is getting ridiculous. I saw you running from the man with the dogs through the cobweb air with the bloody miller's Liverpool scarf flailing behind you like the vaporised graves of forgotten witnesses.

Awake. A wake. A Finlayson double–take.

1+1=1
COMA US
BOTOSUS
~Laza
fish!
He
LIVER
228

Arise. A rose. A ray of hope
A Rutger Hauer.
A replicant repose.

The one matched to one, making the only one who knows where the
sun never sets, and the artists are free to waste anything their miskatonic
minds can conjure.

If the toilet's blocked
Use a plunger.
If the gates are locked,
Form a posse and help the septuagenarians ride into their permanent sun-
rise
– froze in a wooden carving of the garden of Eden.

"We just googled recipes
which you can put weed in."

TEN OF SWORDS

Hour One – Kether

The Marquis woke at five.

Out of sorts.
Cotton–mouthed. Rancid and sequestered. Hungover, beleaguered, un-
crowned and tamed. His divine creative will munching on a lint centred
cough sweet.
He was that he was, his will ventures to repeat, "Get up! Stand up! On
your feet!"
Repeat.
Feet!
The small blind burns the cards over the sink, a small test of god's own
creation. She's wearing somebody else's eyes so you can never see her
winking. The ashes of the cards bitter in the kether you are drinking.

Hour two – Chockmah

From nothing comes nothing till you twist that demon's tawdry skull and
force him drop his bible. An ego felch; a lion's tongue licking the scaly skin
off the industry of religion.
But good coffee first lest intelligence jail me.
It's early yet.
Big hands don't fail me.
Your jackboot left beside my bed; your high heel shoe stuck in my ear;
your lip tattoo, fearful contradictions, your plastic–peopled universe of 'I
heart porno' maledictions.
But coffee first, lest intelligence jail me.
It's only six.
Big feet don't fail me.

Bezbožný milenec
WILL BLOG YOU TO BITS!
GOD DIDN'T MAKE LITTLE GREEN APPLES
AN END TO THE INDUSTRY OF RELIGION
NO.1
NEJTEPLEJŠÍ
Peta NK

Hour three – Binah

Thank you for understanding and not bleeding in the school hallway. Your cassock absorbed the worst of it and your vessel deep and still but for the odd drip drip drip from your funny headless torso.
I hate alarms, firearms, exercise, dogs and worms
And earache even more so.
I braided all my mannequins and named each and every one.
Lisa and Mary to name but two,
And Jo and Mike and Tom.
To see us you would think us mad, but in madness lies our reason.
Return to me, my honey child, for this dark and lonely season.

Hour four – Chesed

Thank you for having me. I didn't mean to wake you. But the sun is rising over the mountain, and it looks so beautiful from here. I made us coffee. Come and sit with me on the roof and we can watch the sun rising together.

You don't want to? You feel sick? You want to sleep a little longer? You feel sharp pains all over your body? Shall I call a doctor? You don't want a doctor? Can I get you anything? You don't want the coffee? You DO want the coffee! I can bring it to you. We can watch the sun rise tomorrow. You don't want to watch the sun rise? Why wouldn't someone want to watch a sunrise? Are you right in the head? You have a pain in your head? Sharp pains? Good.

Hour five – Geburrah

The Marquis threw back the heavy covers of his sandy bed and stretched. "Why me?" he muttered. His bones sun–bleached.
Plucking feathers from his teeth, he lisped, "The Phoenix was under-cooked and should have been stuffed."

God is not great and didn't make little green apples
God, who is dog–spelt, cornered the Marquis and said, "Get up and dance, motherfucker. The dernisáž is gonna be as spectacular as the vernisáž is gonna be as spectacular as the dernisáž is gonna be as spectacular as the vernisáž is gonna be as spectacular as the dernisáž is gonna be as spectacular as the vernisáž ....

Hour six – Tiphareth

Soon his tired eyes took on a noble aspect as he squinted at the horizon.
"There's hope in the old dog yet," he thought as he put his hand down his
pyjama bottoms and wondered whether he shouldn't keep that for later.
There is beauty in compassion and even more beauty in temperance.
This is merely a flesh wound. There's no need for an ambulance.
The opposite chairs icon in perfect symmetry makes a good case for keep-
ing the debate alive and never trusting solutions. The waters are calm. The
air is close. This mood could go either way and the thing is, when you
know, you know. You know?
"No, I know."

Hour seven – Netzach

The Marquis asked her to wear a little less rouge but not to skimp on the
hair spray. He wanted her to be as perfect as perfect. It sucked to be him.
When she leaned in close to whisper 'good night' he had told her in no
uncertain terms that the parameters of the bathtub Sesames, and Bert and
Ernie junkets, were paramount to labelling the unnamed inner elbow and
consequently, Petra, my languishing Tallulah, I'd be grateful if you terra-
formed another empty vessel.
She did not understand his line of thought and so, counting to ten, she
stuck him like a pin cushion till he promised to make sense.

Hour eight – Hod

And oh, the sweet surrender. To let go of the corpulent fox and tie oneself
instead to the dignity, always dignity of six's sincerity. The Talmud burnt
to dust; the coaxing looks, the shy advances pulverised in the labour of
marching hoof to hoof with the fallen angel's brethren whose sole means
of being deciphered is to swear to fuck like a brown antechinus.

Hour nine – Yesod

Overwhelmed by a giantess. The grenade of love unpinned. The founda-
tion of our sacrilege penned by the magic hand of chance. Your unprece-
dented stamina for convoluted pap. Your excuse of being stabbed to death
just so you could take a nap and miss their untimely visit.
The explosion ripped our flesh apart and revealed two lost ventriloquists,
finally free of sexy physicist effigies and the false harmony of contained
conflicts.

Hour ten – Malkuth

Marquis! Marquis! It's nearly three. You wasted half the day away. In fettered looks and cold regards and left to your own devices, you retreated by too many leagues and forgot to feed your dragon. He blazes in the far far east and lights the way for you despite your selfish mornings and pointless solitudes.
Marquis! Marquis! Look at me. The light you never showed is reciprocated evenly by those who loved you despite you never once pretending to show adequate concern about how anyone was faring. Your intellect denying you actual sight visions. Swift and sublime; the reward you sought for doing nought still awaits you in her bosom.
The mother you regarded as a necessary evil.

COINS

ACE OF COINS

**You heard my heart go snap
And you held it together
And you were healthy
And you were there**

I had to start from nothing again

And you were sitting at the starting line with your advice and your energy
"I know that everything changes," you said, in such a way...
In such a way that I thought, "We are definitely going to get naked to-
gether."

"Don't worry about it," you said.
In such a way
that my heart snapped.

You the earth but you the fire the water and the air tied up in a bow in
a gift holding the whole world together (not just me) in a palm full of
raisins and a pentacular look on your
stern
Worn
New
Born
face.

Lovin'
You wis wearin'
the flowers of abundance and all chance beneath your fluttering dress of

eyelids and tempered acquiescence as I mumbled through the pages of your wine, wands and guitariano–shaped swimming pools.

Glasses strewn. Hewn out of whale bones naturally acquired on the muddy shores of youth's promise and the tongue–tied calligraphy of a squirly four–year old just waiting to be five, almost,
almost,
almost
alive.

Cumulative parsecs through the gate of eternal and infinite parsecs divided between Joe Strummer and Billy Bragg, the last gangs in town. Put your monad where your mouth is and give us a revolution before the champagne warms and the fizzy fizz fizzles away.

typing...
typing...
typing...

TWO OF COINS

Clinging upright to five pointed stars there beyond the clear blue sky. My dreams would kill you.

What comes out, goes back in, when you say, 'Thank You'. Everybody knows.

Sing a little louder, Ma; we love it when your voice begins to rattle.
Your country music is so strong and if we are late in the asking, please forgive us our distances.

I woke up this morning with ants in my pants and beans in my sleeves and the waters were rising as the progress of man wrote its first draft on my brow.
Stilled. In infinite sleep. A head full of ideas back–seat–driving me sane, sunlight making good on its promise to help us grow.

Draw back the curtains and look out your window before you set to your breakfast lest you wake the trickster god.

Draft 1 –

We invite you to share your thoughts, stories and works relating to and/or born during these unusual and transformative times. Toss them this way and watch me prance and juggle and tie them tight into a magnificent, large canvas come multi–coloured kite.

Believe that you can make a living flying a kite. Or making kites. Or filming people flying or making kites. Or painting people who film people who make or fly kites. Or make people who fly or make films or kites or films about people who make people who fly or make films or paintings of people who make kites.

The possibilities endlessly tossed up into a ceiling–less space vessel where dreams and ideas materialise as if by swift ocean delivery from the mysterious Amazon occidentally.

I woke up this morning with a grant in my pants and magic beans squirrelled into my molars, to be used with great dexterity to help the homeless and bi–polars.

"Follow the money," she said
As we lay in our conjugal bed.
"I can bend metal with just the power of my mind,"
I said holding her from behind.
"I guess that's a start," she sighed,
Knowing full well that I had lied.
I'll keep her happy with this merry dance
Forever and ever, until I get my chance…

Oodles of light and crowned serpents circle the karmic change of the first breath of a baby.
One for the dealers in daybreak gnosis
One for the bathers with sunburnt toeses

Trust the harmonious flow of nothing into the source at the fork of the river
Dress for success, know you can make it
And when you come to a fork in the river, take it.

Accumulate cigarettes when you are in prison
Spiritualise the material by learning to listen
Caramelise the onions slow as you like
And get more exercise riding a bike

"Work like a sea?
Not uselessly employed,
I might pursue this theme through every change
Of exercise and play, to which the year
Did summon us in its delightful round."

I like a bit of Wordsworth, although I prefer some Ezra Pound.

But
why seperate?

All together now…

Alors tous deux on est repartis
Dans le tourbillon de la vie
On a continué à tourner
Tous les deux enlacés
Tous les deux enlacés.

The cult of the individual inspired to miscarry. The colloquial term for
work these parts 'Guedheembah' (pronunciation Giddy– bah). The 'M'
silent, the 'H' superfluous, the word uplifting, the desire for work embold-
ened.
If you're going to make mistakes, make them right.

Your sentient sapphire booties finding your roots for you, on the grounds
of the self-proclamation that you are worthy. Your hanging tinsel wig en-
tangled in the intimidated earth's rhizomes. The penny farthing was the
way forward.

Quarantine now in the Hope and Anchor more fun than a Costa coffee.
"Is a 'lockdown' more of an aphrodisiac than a picnic in the forest of Ver-
sailles?" you asked me.
"Is my dream of a small farm in the Czech countryside the same as your
dream of a small farm in the Czech countryside?"
One metamorphosed into one, but not the same one.

So you see, in this we must work together.
You analyse and I shall expel.
It's true, the lockdown is good for the blood and sex toys are selling well.

"I'm a poet."
A what?
"I'm the poet."
A cola!
"A poet."
What kind of poet?
"A modern one. You should buy one of my books."

Your poems will last longer than the toys, but the contents of your fridge
are diminishing faster than you can say 'Jeanne Moreau in the arms of a
sissy writer'. Change your clothes. Change your mind. Change your sales
pitch. Be the cola. Don't be the cola. Be both of those things. The cola and
not the cola.
You will leave those dolls and dildos in the dust.

And your real hair rising with the lubricated, feel thin, rubber
leaves of grass.

THREE OF COINS

Only two came to pay their respects when consciousness was buried. Mr and Mrs Bliss written in pictures limited to symbols we have interpreted a priori.

Harpo the Monk leading the Blitz
Chico the Architect bringing the good flowers
Groucho, the master of his art, receiving them both with open arms.
Groucho the gravedigger planting his regard in this dead land.

Bliss is a baby sleeping in your arms.
Blitz is a square and a compass.

The lambskin apron tucked into the pine box at the end of days. A jigsaw puzzle of pure white gloves, no two exactly the same; laid at the locked door of Solomon's Temple by the light of the unlimited all-seeing eye.

The Ashlar rough, perfected.

Labour for the sake of the joy of the chance that the perfect snowflake will finally be recorded. Every branch measured lovingly by a level in permanent flux.
Infinity melting on the palm of your tongue.

Bliss is good food and good company.

Blitz is all catechumens. Good or bad.

Cosmic Consciousness unbuckled and without a care in the world and with a small Spanish guitar which she will produce from beneath her apron towards the end of the evening to impress the party goers. Three! Three! Look at me! I still love you. My fingertips dancing around the base of your cup. Don't cover your eyes! Pull back the veil. Could you make this church look any more like a jail!?

Bliss is a window onto the beach. And the beach.
Blitz is a real rabbit hole in a metaphorical rabbit hole looking for someone solid to sue.

The earthly and the spiritual found within the confines of a mechanical musical planet, wound up by a vagabond misquoting Chomsky with the fervour of a slutty evangelist.

Prioritise the insults from your compromised inner critic. Don't take to heart the poison that flows through his veins. Cauterise the wound when you've chopped the positive reflection of the pilgrim out.

Send him to the red-light district. Take his mind off things. A place where the faithful and the charitable can die in the arms of someone who truly loves what they do. We are all apprentices here. All we ask is one more hour to perfect our trade in decay, and how many more hours are there till judgement day, again?

Blitz is the place where John Lennon was shot.
Bliss is Oscar Peterson on a courageous day in April 2020 when the pandemic subsided in our parallel world, and you got down on your knees and asked me to take you away from all this. Make sense of the senseless and settle for nothing but the best of everything.

Prince Buster pealed his skin off and we fixed that ache in his belly with a remedy so fine
And we set the remedy down on acetate before the drugs kicked in
Then sat back and listened to the pain WE were in
And the pain we were in sounded really really good
So we picked up Cecil's pealed–off–skin and cleaned up all the blood

And the note in the broken sarcophagus read….

If we feel alone, we are really not alone
If we feel sad, we are really not sad
If we feel a feeling, we are really not feeling
If we think a thought, we are really not thinking.

FOUR OF COINS

The laboratory welcomed the young, plump monk.
"What's your pleasure?" the maître d asked.
"The usual," Hanz said.

"We have new vaccines," the maître d said.
"I won't be needing any of your new vaccines," the monk replied.
"But what of the new viruses?"
"I'll take my chances. Besides, I have quite a few prayers here of my own."
Then the maître d asked the monk, "Do you believe in God?"
"There is no such thing," the monk said.
"As God?" the maître d asked.
"No such thing as your question," the monk replied.

Don't hold on so tight to your talent. You don't deserve any of your grant-ed wishes or such an easy way out. Take time to scatter what you have gathered. Shuffle. Then shuffle again. Never assume anything of anyone or anything. Shuffle, and in turn let your talents shuffle you.
And above all avoid repetition.
Having said that, don't be afraid to switch back to the chorus of your own number any time you fancy.

And love the secret Ska boy in his shades; the evaporating stage dancer drawn from a memory; the clean-fingered shoplifter passing without a glance, her thoughts and plans and stolen jewellery in her hand in her bag

in her coat pockets; Black Francis unrecognised, glad of his anonymity; Billy Bragg texting his Mum, forgot he left the house with his Harry Potter slippers on and the glint in your eye, hidden by your own sunglasses extends to the tips of your lips pursed because you did spy the one girl in the street whose question rings true.
"How much is that doggy in the window and would he want to run away if I bought him?"

You can take all of this home with you, but you won't. I know you, and you know where your next meal is coming from, and you just don't want to let yourself down and your mother always told you – Do what you know. Do what works. Do what pays. Do what others do.
She shuffled you well then laid you out on a huge garden tableaux and glued you the way she spread you. You looked so beautiful in your cute little booties and mittens and freshly ironed uniform.

And you, you look so beautiful sitting there working on your new Jerusalem, slowing down time with your transitory intercourse and convoluted dreamscapes, all feedback carnations, torn jeans, washboard and frottoir as you pick up the beat with the machine gun energy you save for me and the theatre. Crushing it like an aspirin in the late late supper of your clay–faced, pigeon toed, small handed nemeses.

Your letter to a world in crisis.

Hold on. Don't give up. I am here for you. I got four John the Baptiste heads. Got the first one cheap from the Irish Film Centre. 5 punts back in the day. I had to pay through the nose for the others.
And like some insatiable cornball Salome, you asked me to purchase a fifth. It occurred to me that five John the Baptiste heads is too many John the Baptiste heads. And then it occurred to me that at least three of the heads I already owned must, by definition of 'John the Baptiste head', be fake! If not all four!
A fifth might be the only way to guarantee I own the real one.
And now I am really not sure of myself or my possessions. Same thing in this instance.
It's my lack of faith in what I have and my desire to be sure by what I will/ may have that distances me from you.

If I could just have paid more attention when I had but one head. Proved that that was the real one. Then I might be closer to fixing you. But hold on, world. Don't give up.
I got four John the Baptiste heads to be going on with. That will at least buy us some time till Pozzo arrives with his science, and jibes and bucket full of Jesus teeth.

Looking at the yucca with a critical eye.
If you don't water the yucca, the yucca will die.
If you paint the yucca and the painting sells,
Remember guests and fish emit similar smells.
When artists and poetry forget to rebel.

And you paint yucca after yucca after yucca after yucca, so the beauty is diluted and weakens the spell. One of each, we must learn, is ample.
"Now, may I use your toilet?"
"Yes, for example."

The nice man at the laboratory sat the young plump monk at his table.
"Will you be dining alone tonight, sir?"

"Certainly," the monk said.

And so, the maître d handed the keys of the lab to the monk and held a minute's silence for every domestic cat and outdoors person who had died of coronavirus. Sixty-nine days passed and so did the monk.

"Death," the maître d reflected "The only true form of spontaneous solidarity."

And the whole time, the monk hadn't once asked what the numbered doors in the lab were for or where they lead?

The cinema organ riddler chef hero fighter motorcycle ghost shoots his blanks into the sky which catches the stranded, male actor's eye. His dream King Lear script dropped in a puddle. With no fourth point there could be no middle.

Now dare to dare – Don't play it safe

Be the person you always wanted to be

FIVE OF COINS

I'm not going to start without you. Not till you deliver a killer line to me. Everyone knows how much a first line counts and I count on you.

Oh, for christ's sake. Why so quiet? So suddenly. For Christ's sake. You keep it to yourself. Make us all feel guilty. That magnificent guilt. That Kafkaesque guilt.
Would you rather be with Ted? Would you rather be dead? Would you rather there wasn't a word for anything? I sometimes wish there wasn't a word for anything but then where would my great first line come from?

As we sit in the car together in the rain and both of us see the lady who we know for sure died last week. We see her get out of her car in the rain and walk into the bakery on the other side of the street. We have willed ourselves into the uncomfortable silence we have, each of us, soliloquised about all these years.

And you grunt. And I grunt.
"Can you believe what you are seeing! Can you believe it!"
We calm down. We both understand that neither of us can believe it and we both understand that neither of us have an answer for what we are witnessing. And so, we stop grunting.

I dare you to tell me what I'm thinking. I double dare you.
Book without borders.
Quotidian the life of the aimless deutan. A poem without colours. Mademoiselle Winter, sell me your ear; you said you could get me a job at your

publishing house. I hereby send you my heart. I fancy a change and you look so pretty. A word without borders is ALL words. I love you all. I'm going on strike. We may not eat for a month, but at least we may grunt at our opposition; at human labour; together.

You held me up.
You pulled my hair back.
We kept tabs on our feelings.
Julie Christie nerves jangle.
P–Orridge connected.

Searching the bins in the empty park for the right type of emotion. Using those walking sticks healthy hikers use. You sit still and alone when you can, but you don't ever need to.
Your tall thin ghost in hand–me–down jodhpurs, geeing you on with what little reserves she has reserved.
"I was only ever thinking of you. I did everything for you."
You resent her.
This altruism.

The shadows of the branches of the two naked elms form the skeleton of a laughing child on the sidewalk in front of the church.

A pristine abandoned shopping trolley.
A children's charity lady with clipboard and portal.
A feeling of having been here before before.
Home soon to the Holly Hop and the nightly spin of the Wheel.
Fighting above my weight.
Best way to improve oneself they say.
Meanwhile I get the living shit kicked out of me till I learn my bloody lesson.

A pissing cyclist in lycra.
A wishing woman in debt.
A bottomless woman wishing well.
A diamond ankle bracelet.
I feel so old.

"This pain you feel inside. This pain which does not belong to you. Remember you have taken it from others. Remember who you have taken it from. You made your choice. You did it out of love. Offering to take on another's load is more than a polite, honed, verbal gesture of comradeship.

It is to put yourself in the firing line, away from your comfort food and Grandfather's chest full of antique Samurai swords.

The only respite you can rely on at this moment in time is the quiet release of your well-earned tears. You will never be alone as long as you feel this much pain and this much love.
Are you ready for the time of your life? That portal you carry around your neck; that electronic symbol of hope will teleport and transmogrify your people.

Beautiful agony. Hard won ecstasy. The best type.
You can't take your dough when you go.
Power to the person!
Shall we have pasta tonight?

SIX OF COINS

Bicyclebicycle. Bicyclebicycle. Bicyclebicycle.

"You have to smile or you would cry."
"You mean laugh."
"No, I mean cry!"
"No, I mean you don't mean 'smile', you mean 'Laugh'. The saying is, 'You have to laugh or you would cry.'"
"That's what I said."
"You didn't. You said 'smile'."
"Yes."
"Yes what?"
"You have to smile."

Anyway

Which planet do you want to stop off at first? I got the recorded scunds of all six on this new app called 'Fureur de Vivre' in exchange for just one juicy blue rose case.
Troubling abstractions being the fuel of spontaneous magnanimity.

Grunt.
Grunt.
The moment of truth.

Success! You gave away all but your dreams. The third part of your three part puzzle, the bottomless frame of a rowing boat.
Venus first. Bright and beautiful. I hold my arms out, like this, and I am ready to catch her, I think. Pull the plug on the sound effects. Make her laugh.

Success! She laughed.

Ahhh, here we are, you magical man, you! Oh, how we enjoyed your bon
mots, your reparte, your já nevím.
But remember, you are here for me. Be horrible to other women.

Your dream. Not mine.
I hatemyselfIhatemyselfIhatemyself…
ENOUGH!
Diplomatic immunity broadens the mind.

I got my wounds in my sleep.
All I own is yours to keep.

Don't mean no harm.
The party is swinging.
The participants are modest

And the christ man is drinking – nightly.
Now
The social's unclothed.
Our sweatpants and t–shirts
Darwinia–volved.

Dangerous ice–creams.
"The state he's in!"
Put out the fire.
Murder sin.

I was aggressive.
Now I've given up.
I tried to be cool, but now, I've given up.
I wore a goddamn suit!
I've given up.
I met your Mum.

It's easier now.

No suit. No cool. No aggression.
Just one homo sapien and another homo sapien and a reason to be living.
And when you feel like you can't do anything right. When you feel like
everything you do just pisses the people you love off. When you feel like
you are trying your best, but your best is considered to be an insult to those
around you.
Grunt.
When you find yourself apologising for everything you say or are feeling
chastised after everything you have said, and you feel sick in your chest
and the pain is unbearable and you can't understand how you are taken to
be such a despicable person.
Grunt.
Remember...
All the good stuff you ever look for or continue to look for in books and
in nature and art and in culture IS there. Remember that.

Know when to let the Empress go. She is used to being alone. She can
handle herself. And she does. Admirably. But if you see her breaking down,
remember she was there for you always. She would drop everything for
you in a heartbeat to pick you up, see that you got back on your feet and
could once again summon up the energy to howl at the moon with her.
Gather your sticks and pay your respects to your silent partners who work

tirelessly to defeat the all-powerful, badly scripted, terrifying, indiscriminate 'nothing' and pay careful attention to the hurtful details. Don't ignore the hurtful details. The cards, which at first you don't understand, or actively despise are the cards which love you the most.

"Life is like riding a skateboard. To keep your balance, you must keep moving."
"Bicycle."
"What?"
"Bicycle. Bicycle. Don't look at me like that. Bicycle."
"Why are you saying the word bicycle at me?"
"Because you got the quote wrong. It's 'Life is like a bicycle.' Einstein said it. Skateboards hadn't been invented when he said it."
"Why would he say skateboards then?"

"He didn't he said bicycle! Bicycle.......

SEVEN OF COINS

"After another "Hard Day's Night" and not one text from me loved one,

I look on me werk and think, 'What's the friggin' point?'"

And then I remember…

I remember that blue tits are my favourite garden bird, and that when I see them I feel lighter.
They have absorbed the dark lessons I have learnt and pulverised them with their cheeky, yellow insouciance. I could trust you, tits, if you shared your hyperlink to the thunderbird totem your worshippers built in the field I tilled and the ground I paved and the air I breathed, which is all I need when I recall how the great curator made connections between our projects of Wonderdust, love and angry, sequinned glamour.

I remember those were newgirl–shapes in the clouds and the days and nights and the baby's cries and man has been to the depths of the ocean and the depths of the earth and I can see into the past with my new fish eyes and condoms full of Fanta/Coke–crystal balls and the guilt I felt for not telling you everything I was working on while I was working on it and the power of the sound of the Bang and Olufson speakers my millionnaire newwoman bought for me and I turned them into garden furniture so I could sit there in the morning, watch the rising sun and with my powerful pocket binoculars spot our cute little companions praying wordlessly in colours to the freaks who made us.

Here, I remember choosing my mode and then changing my mode and then going back and then giving up and then soldiering on and then making money and then not making money and then peeking over the mound of sand you buried me in up to my neck and spying the exact outfit I think

کلثوم نوا میں خاور حیات
۰۰

would make me look stunning and capture the essence of who I want to be seen to be.
The 'M' Path. A jollier Roger.

I put my footprints all over this rolling limestone and recorded my demos with the full blood of a strong, black–haired pirate.
Purposefully planted Persian psychedelics as Farsi as the eye can see.
And the deep, blue sea has its eye on me.

I remember the well-dressed dustman with a fetish for mismatched bobby socks and breakfast in bed with the dead.

I remember all the teachers and how online we shouldn't speak when another student is talking and how even a sneeze can disrupt the whole class, and but if just but how when everything has been done by somebody else, you still have to do it all by yourself.

And look back at what you have done. Is it just my style or do you all give up easy too?

Pluck one. Go on. The blue tits got plenty of secrets left. Pop it under your tongue and wait thirty minutes. You'll see. But first let's rid you of that melancholy. Here, try this on for size. Those old robes ain't fitting for someone with your lust for living. Who could possibly even imagine what's going on in that wonderful head of yours if you insist on dressing like a hobo.

The borders may be closed but a bird's still got standards.
And the light shines on the pink halo made flesh.

Elpsis Boo.
Elpsis Boo.

And the turquoise of your tights match the colour on the cheeks of the ice people when they blush.
But you are far from home, even on your hard-earned patch of land.
Now pluck again,
from your own resources,
turn, turn, turn,
to no one but yourself
and try your best not to let love give in to pain.

Dear radiant Canadian Ornithologist,

I hereby step back. Know thus far forth – You must drop that dog–eared exercise book of yours to the floor.
Your C.V. is writ. Be satisfied that the balloon creatures you harvested are there for your benefit, and maybe if they call for a ceasefire of every warring faction, or else widen the pandemic, the musketeers will stay home with their loved ones and, on reflection, weighing up the pros and cons, settling down and eating potatoes and freshly understood quark soup.
Never
murder
again.

Elpsis Boo

Born
Educated
Worked

And what did my work serve me? And should I have been doing what I was doing all that time? And does it matter? And does it matter if it matters?
And how does it work that sad chords and sad notes played on an instrument can make you cry? And how come when we find what we want, we don't want to let go of it? Not even for a second. Not ever. It's a curse.

Nature, dear Elpsis, has its own way of wanting us too.
The tears in my eyes are for us all.

Elpsis Boo Hoo

Born
Educated
Worked
Tended the weeds in his modest, modern garden plot
Held modest hands
Held his head above the tempest
and when he died, he left behind a message for the newgardener who would be being there.

The message he left blank, to give the next dodo a fighting chance.

EIGHT OF COINS

Make me a nice song about foot, head or traces
Read me a bedtime story

Make me a beautiful poem about problems which make all the problems go away
To plumb such depths except for the sake of poetry is unforgivable indulgence.

Lorne learns to live. Not to produce. But to leave 'produce'. To make nice.

Sleeping head to toe. Waking with feet in the sky. The sun in my eyes.
The pied constellation blowing my tiny mind.
And to my best friend I say, 'Always a pleasure, never a chore.'
Because

Always a song for you,
Always a story for you,
Always a beautiful poem for you

Five segments of a fruit you taught me
Five petals of a flower you bought me
Five and five making it hard for me not to care, when my hat is in the sinking sand and my shoes are in the toxic air.

Dear Prudence, there is strength in doing nowt.

When five toes and five can go back to work again and overthrow all the governments and run faster than the speed of light dead easy and you can get rid of that nasal whine and the desire to say hydrate instead of drink

water and when there are no more rotting horses in our fake zoo soup glue and no more soup on our pristine white self-cleaning suits and no more suits that don't fit like a dream and no more human beanz asking what does it mean. Then I'll be happy.
Until then you can hide here as long as you want.

I have so many songs
I have so many stories

And so many poems about problems which make having problems seem that much more shareable, but they don't solve the problems. A problem is there like bad weather. It is a rhizomatic conglomeration of forces which are not all under our control and we must learn to live with them. Believing that the thunderstorm is not the result of an upset super being is a start.

So,
Get your nose to the grindstone
Move your nose away from the grindstone

Make nose friendly grindstones. They can do that. As soon as your pink flesh touches the machinery the thing automatically switches off. Saves noses.

I wish I were eight people and there were eight days in the week and that there were eighty hours in the day and that the sun would come inside and stay inside and take off its kinky boots and lie in bed next to us like three big shaggy mountain dogs and there's all the food we like in the fridge and I memorised every single word I ever read and could recite them all back to you verbatim if I wanted to but would rather play the dark blue and then white and then light blue and then black dilated pupil game in protective orange choruses built to keep me focused till I end my symphony with plenty more energy to spare for my favourite Sutras, sandwiches and meditations.

Words? What words? Repeat the words? Why repeat the words?

Make sure the black of the black tie matches the black of the black suit jacket and that the light blue of the carpenter's eyes is the same as the view of the blue of the sea on the globe from the depths of space.

And when the subject of words comes up at the meeting and everyone tilts their head towards you, don't forget to flash those creamy pegs of white and your funeral eyes of brilliant blue.

Perseverance. Repetition. Why repeat perseverance? How repeat?

There, there, there, yes, don't stop, there, there, there

Yessss.

NINE OF COINS

I been playing it cool with you, Nine of Pentacles, but enough's enough. I've decided to tell it like it is.

You're a street cop taps her fingers to N.W.A. and Public Enemy in the renovated Oldsmobile with your enervated partner who you would lay

down your precious life for. Your partner who is to culture what British Stilton is to French Steak. You two cool girl guides learnt to take Mahler in your flat feeted, free thinking, well considered strides and now can floor a giant with just an intelligent look. Learnt to bathe in asses' milk without letting the asses' milk curdle and worked your way to the top by being smart enough to ask the Great Eagles to take you all the way to Mordor.

I used to be intimidated by your honesty.
I used to be intimidated by your education.
Now I just want to be you.

I want to look like you, see like you, think like you.
I know that this is how you want it, number nine. I know this because you didn't get where you are today without becoming the others who thrilled and appalled and delighted you.

And as the nearness of you is not enough, the nearness of your inspirations was never enough for you either. You metamorphosed into those you loved and your wildest dreams came true.

You achieved all this by taming the beast inside. The fake you. The bad Coop'. The bad The Trial.
So, I'm giving myself a break. I am going to enjoy this.

Darker lighter darker lighter
Deeper darker lighter lighter lighter

Saw every episode of Happy Days and despite his open heterosexual love of the Fonz, he never owned a leather jacket – or wait, no, he did, for one afternoon. But it was a second–hand jacket he bought. He took it home and his grandmother pointed out to him that it was a lady's jacket. And you know how you know? It zips the other side. This put your father off the whole idea of leather. Took it back to Affleck's Palace. Suede for him from then forever.

Hand touches head – Head thinks better of it – Hand comes down – Then where is it supposed to go?
Your dress is made of adverts – but the adverts which predate the need for advertisers. Chew on that one, you sneezy, corporate tit–shrinkers.

I deserve you.
We tell myself I deserve you.

But this time! This time it's true.
I do deserve the very best.

And I gather the stars you walked on to be here, and you think it's funny
and strange ,but I solemnly swear there is nothing I wouldn't do for you.
You got me under your spell and my my my what a wonderful day and just
listen to all the guests. This really is one hell of a garden party. Nothing cli-
ché, very arty. I see revolutions on your shoulder pads and German philos-
ophers in your sandals, and blithe spirits pace back and forth making small
talk in your shrubbery, disciplining camera–shy faeries splashing around
in your make–believe water features, praising the host for her foresight
and independence and enviable sensitivity.

Go ahead and smile. Watch interviews with other artists you admire.
Learn from them. Copy them. Kill them.
Larger Brighter Larger Brighter
Deeper Larger Brighter Brighter Brighter

I'm in love with you
I'm in love with you
I'm in love with you

And I'm going to be a paperback writer.

TEN OF COINS

You beside me, sighing in the wilderness.

No more unnecessary tears.
No more unnecessary laughter.
Cliches have no impact.

Wands are lying forgotten in the real gone grass.
The wicked witch rests in peace beneath the wisteria.

Beetles coupling in the shade of wine lipped plastic picnic beakers.
New life being breathed into the immortal verses sung by our toothsome
friends full of sympathy and tomato bread.

Here is the gate to the magician's enclave. The alien on the bough. A sense
of loss. A tiny death. And decadence is as decadence does. It endures.
No more unnecessary pain. Unless that's the reason you came. What you
do with your wealth now is your own business.

A bustling state – A telepath – Arthur Dent with a peppering of St Ford
Prefect; both heads easing into their emerald-green bosom–pillows – All
gratuitous violence renounced. Stay away from the naked nuns, and the
geraniums.

Don't buy guns. Be a gnu.

And here we will stay. Here we will grow old.

When your peculiar impulses have been normalised and your picnic salad leaves reduced to mush we will transcend nature and seek an alchemist who fits our skin–tight budget and confiscate his rolled-up bank notes and harems of Rubenesque Skywalkers.

The drums of the townsfolk beat a Gaelic cadence to an elusive Tarot-toraT synonym relying on the Liddypool shuffle to replenish the hearts they squandered on their half–arsed, quarter–baked, three–titted money making schemes.

Under no circumstances trust anyone if they deal in ultimatums. Including you. The wise know that you are called upon to be at the service of forgetfulness and permanent change. Penitence shall not be rewarded. 'Quiet' and 'Industrious' is only acceptable if the pleb knows how to dance without moving their cold–sore lips.

We are all accused. We all use words which presuppose our guilt.

So come down from the pulpit. The pulpit has herpes since the cleaner spent too long at the fleas in the doorkeeper's collar. Though the scripture is unalterable, the listener is not. The lobster is. The corpse is not. Death is the ten blank canvases and birth their fluffer brides.

The travelling player corpses at the funnier lines; cock–eyed mercury delivering more than behaviour and speech now that the restrictions are being lifted.
We depart to the next village in buckets riddled with holes. Sudden steps. Soul–sick pancake–shaped spaceships dropping care packages on the illest planets, and straw and axes and stones and water and grim but cool gothic My Little Ponies.

Don't pretend you're in control. Not without the help of family and friends; and who will be your family and who will be your friends? Well, that's for me to know and for you to find out.

Put your faith in eternal doubt and scissors and fresh fruits and dentists. And dreams of dentists. And dreams of crypts made of teeth which dentists could not save, but the choreless alchemist had time to collect and fashion into something we could all enjoy for the same price as the most modest rhinoplasty, wind dried puffin or major league baseball game played in actually Amerika.

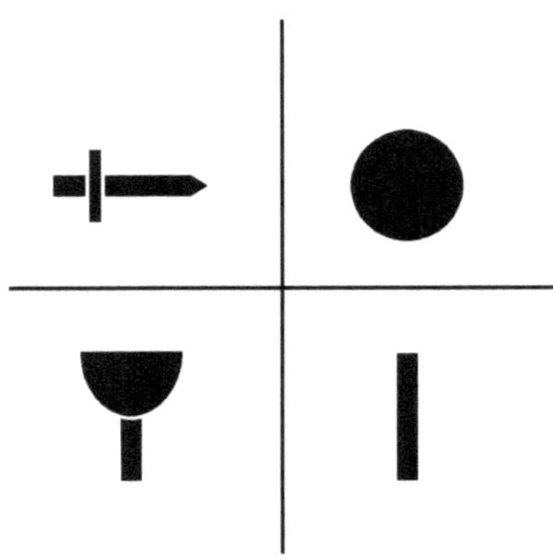

AFTERWORD

Infinite thanks to you Jo Blin, for gifting me with my first Tarot pack, for helping me to finish this book, and for designing and literally putting this book together. Thanks to you Lusi Lu, for gifting me with my first Marseille pack and all the Jungian synchronicities that followed. Plus a huge thank you to my high school English teacher, Miss Mellor, for introducing me to the big three - T.S. Eliot, Samuel Beckett and James Joyce. Thanks to you too, Chantelle Goldthwaite, for inspiring and encouraging me to continue writing about paintings; your own collages being the first of which I felt an irresistible compunction to have some literary fun with.

I do not want to go into too much detail about the process of creating my own Tarot pack or of the writing of the book, except to say that each card was written as a separate entity with conscious connections to its fellow Arcana. The card suits, in and of themselves, encourage thematic structure, but this never tied any one card to its neighbour without those ties coming spontaneously and naturally in accordance to their own numerological and symbolic values.

The images I chose for each card came fast. The arduous task of comparing my own images' symbolism with the Crowley/Harris, Rider/Waite/Smith and Marseille packs, revealed connections so close to the classic meanings of the cards that it is now hard for me to imagine that the paintings I painted, sometimes ten/twelve years previously, were not always intended for this very end.

To say such a thing might seem mildly hysterical, but it brings up one of the most important things I would like to say about my own personal relationship with Tarot. To read the cards one must open up to the belief that everything is a metaphor for everything else. The Tarot tells YOUR story if you let it. The Tarot KNOWS you. The Tarot IS everyone. To say that a spread can be twisted in any way, to anybody, to mean anything you want it to is not a criticism of the Tarot, it is the Tarot's strength.

A good reader will indicate to the querent the symbols available in front of them and the links cards may have with each other, leaving the querent to decide what significance these images have to them.

THANKS TOO TO

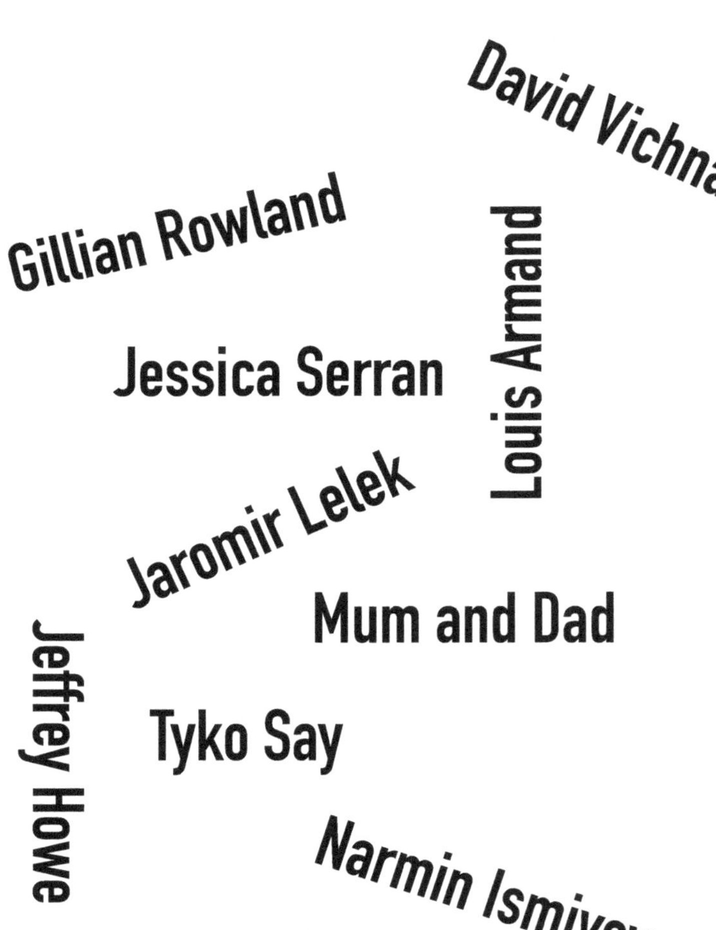